Reddaren Academic Publishing

New York - London - Madrid - Paris - Hong Kong - Tokyo

All rights reserved. 2021. ISBN 979-8704735304

Reddaren Academic Publishing is committed to a sustainable future for our business, our readers, and our planet. This book is printed on demand and is available in electronic format.

Science Fiction Stories Beyond Normal

Roland E. Fielding

THE FIGHT FOR THE GODDESS

Seras took cover while trying to fix the hand canon attached to his arm. The gruesome scene wouldn't have been out of place in the nightmares of a madman. Everywhere he looked he could see his comrades giving their best to defeat the faceless monsters that had decided to invade their world that particular day. Floating blobs with spikes that protruded from different places. Those monsters had no other mission than to invade and colonize planets by the sheer force of their numbers. A grotesque form of life whose only intent was to bring chaos to a world of order. Luckily, the alarm systems had offered plenty of time to prepare against their arrival and Seras together with his company had organized a defense strategy that offered several layers of cover and protection. Everything about those warriors made it perfectly clear that they had been born for battle. They shined in war. They craved it as if it were the very thing that gave a clear purpose to their existence.

"Two of them are headed towards the second line through that corner!" Said Lieutenant Jeqq while readjusting his scope. "The second line has tagged them, Lieutenant. I am heading there myself", replied a female voice with the confidence of being part of an undefeated battalion. Corporal Ladia had a keen eye to spot the possible moves of the enemy before they occurred. Her personal skills combined perfectly with the strategies of her battalion: Always leave a seemingly weaker spot to attract the enemies to it in order to concentrate the fire power in a smaller area. The initial ground granted to them made it seem like the best option to keep pushing in that area, creating a bottleneck where any shot was certain to impact one target or another. The red amorphous walls surrounding the battlefield glistened with the shots directed towards the two blobs that had deviated from their group. Had they been more numerous, the attempt could have certainly opened a second front, thus making the battle unnecessarily longer than it should have been.

After a few excruciatingly long instants, Seras managed to fix and reload his hand canon and directed it towards the last remaining group of assailants that, despite their losses, maintained their attack as if retreat wasn't an available option for them. That mindless devotion for chaos would have shattered many, but the Defense Battalion 407 were outstandingly efficient answering that violent madness with cold efficient destruction. In the right flank of the front, Ladia finished the fallen enemies with a double shot, as it was her habit. The close-range shots had the particular advantage of burning organic tissue at a better rate than shots with the scope from afar.

"You fought well today. However, your hand canon seems to be malfunctioning, kid. You know the protocol. Prepare for examination at the appointed spot". Lieutenant Jeqq had pronounced the words through the communicator as if they weren't attached to the disturbing effects that failing the inspection would carry. Failing would have meant certain termination for being a defective part of an otherwise perfect defense machine that could not allow nor ignore failure. Seras sent an affirmative signal but pronounced no further words. Saying something would have shown weakness, fear, or a desire to remind everyone of his services in the 407 in order to inspire solidarity, or worse yet: pity. The soldiers in the defense battalion were expected to fulfill their duties regardless of previous service and merits. Each battle was the first one, and each foe could be the last one if underperformance was allowed to evolve into failure. What benefit would there be in a soldier who can't fight, a canon that can't shoot, or an officer who can't lead?

The cold efficiency of a system improved through countless cycles and generations of warriors left no place for those who felt short of what was necessary to protect The Goddess. That religious faith impregnated every aspect of a warrior's life in that place. The Goddess was everything. She was around you, she was you, and you were part of her. The Goddess was their universe itself and each living creature belonging to it. Invaders had to be destroyed, battles had to be fought, and the sacred duty of protecting The Goddess had to be carried out passing the torch from generation to generation.

Ladia stared at Seras wishing with all her being that his partner could avoid termination and they could still fight many more battles together. She had entered the service a bit earlier than him, and she had been responsible for part of his training. She remembered those sessions where every practice shot and every move slowly and consistently forged the new recruit into the flawless combat asset that was now only a couple of battles away from becoming a corporal like herself. It was inevitable to doubt their whole existence if after all those efforts, a failing hand canon could end the life of such a promising soldier. Even in her adamant devotion to the protection of The Goddess she sometimes wished that such episodes could finish in a more humane way. Rewarding devotion with death once a soldier was no longer useful seemed somewhat unfair to her, but as many other things, the reasons behind such protocols and procedures were above her station. Who was she or anyone else around to question a system that had kept them alive and well for generations upon generations? It wasn't easy to doubt such efficient work of interconnections, but at that precise moment she was just a warrior worried about a comrade. She sent Seras a heart by the communicator. "Hm... I'm getting there" was his short and enigmatic answer.

On his way towards the assigned point for evaluation, Seras slowed down just enough to contemplate the landscapes around him for a moment. From the moist surfaces to the endless movement of different beings performing some important task, everything seemed alien and at the same time it made him feel at home, and part of something bigger than himself. If he had been born in a different category... How different would his life have turned out? His pending evaluation had made him more aware of his existence than ever before. Under an endless highway of weird creatures moving here and there to keep that planet running. Everyone and everything seemed to have its place, except for himself at this moment.

"Worried, aren't you?" The mysterious figure addressed Seras taking him out of his grim thoughts for an instant. "My first evaluation" was his short, yet informative answer. "Ah... Yes, one can hardly blame you for being nervous when so much is at stake, hah?" The man was wearing a uniform from a special unit that was easy to identify by number, but difficult to describe in essence. All those different special units looked alike, and all of them had too specific tasks to keep track on what all of them did or had done. Some of those teams spent their lives training for specific enemies that might never appear, but having them ready to fight was a guarantee of success in the face of any and all eventualities.

"It kinda makes you wonder, doesn't it?" Continued the man. "We give so much and the moment they are done with us, death is our only reward". Seras observed the man with careful attention. His words sounded true, but he was pronouncing them without the necessary conviction to take them seriously. "Imagine if we could be free to be who we really are? Wouldn't that be better than this life of service and death? Let me show you something... Give me your hand..." The man offered his hand together with a smile that was too suspicious and malign to leave any room for second guesses. Seras charged his hand canon and ordered the man to step away from him. "What are you so afraid of? I offer you my hand and you answer me with the threat of violence? There is obviously something wrong with you, and perhaps your evaluation is..." Seras shot the man right in the lower part of his body and recharged for a second finishing shot. "The stench of your corruption can be felt from the distance. I have no idea how you managed you stay alive unnoticed for so long, but this ends here and now for you. Any last words?" The man looked at Seras with as much hatred as he could possibly muster and tried to grab him one last time with one of his mutated tentacles. "Together we are stronger! There will be many more like me! There is no escape from..." Seras finished the man with a second shot that obliterated what was left of him, and deactivated his weapon knowing full well what was about to happen next.

Instants after he stepped away from the remains of the dead man, a cleaning team appeared accompanied by an evaluator wearing an impressive uniform that included a battle coat indicating his guild and function. The scene would have been difficult to explain under other circumstances, but with some remaining tissue available for inspection, the cleaning team would soon clear things up.

"Weapon deactivated? Good. You know the drill. Let me see that hand canon while the cleaners do their thing. You are that soldier from the 407 right? My evaluation is with you". The man seemed to have the habit of answering his own questions, so the whole conversation felt more like a monologue for Seras. "It malfunctioned during my last battle. I am set for clearance or extermination", explained Seras trying to fake an air of acceptance for the prospect of his own end. Evaluator Hato began his procedures and quickly mustered a smile.

"There's nothing wrong with your hand canon. At least nothing that can't be repaired. In a few moments it will be as good as new". The cleaning team gave their assessment about the organic remains on the floor through the communicator and the Evaluator felt compelled to share them with Seras. "When did you realize that guy had been corrupted?" Seras tried to contain the surprise for how the whole situation had turned out. He went quickly from the stressful prospect of his own death, to the relief of knowing his hand canon would be operational soon without further consequences for him. "Our officers train us to recognize signs and symptoms of corruption, sir, but you already know that". The Evaluator looked at the kid amused by the boldness of his last remark. "I certainly know about your training, soldier, but you acted quickly and decisively back there. It should make us all proud that the new generation of defense forces are as capable to recognize threats as you have proven yourself to be".

Seras looked at the man. His words seemed honest and his expression showed no signs of a condescending effort. "I decided to shoot him after seeing one of his small tentacles uncovered by the sleeve when he offered his hand". Hato nodded in agreement ratifying the soldier's good call. "You know, it takes very little to get infected by those things. One wrong step and you become one of them. But they are smart... they know our ways. They are aware of how easy it would be for us to exterminate them if they infected too many people too fast".

Seras became concerned. The prospect of that type of corruption spreading throughout the land could be the end of his world. The end of The Goddess. "Listen up soldier. It takes courage to make the right choice and stare in the face of corruption without flinching. Your service will not go unnoticed! By the powers invested in me by the directorate, I hereby promote you to the rank of corporal for your extraordinary performance today". The young soldier, now corporal, stood there surprised and slightly mistrustful, until the lines in his uniform's collar and shoulders abruptly changed colors. "I don't think I..." The Evaluator interrupted Seras: "Don't try to sound humble or coy with me, boy. You know as well as I do that you were one or two battles away from earning this promotion anyway. Go back to the 407 and keep up the good work. The Goddess must be protected! Everything for The Goddess!" "Everything for The Goddess" answered Seras in turn. Once he had moved far enough from the scene with the cleaners and the Evaluator, the young corporal began to breathe heavily and felt his legs shaking. He had been two steps away from death and, despite his unquestionable bravery, anyone would have felt their knees trembling after such rollercoaster of emotions.

The society he had grown up in was full of painful contradictions. On the one hand they valued commitment and devotion to The Goddess, but on the other hand they showed a cold impersonal disregard for others once they were unable to perform their function in that society. The contrast was harsh, and it had created the perfect grounds for secretive rebel movements that refused to accept the way things were. Seras and many others might have understood their position, but having rogue elements around trying to mutate others against their will to further their cause was something no defense force would ever tolerate. For countless generations the pleas of the rebels had been met with violent retaliation. They had been branded as a source for chaos and destruction, and even if at some point their cause was justified, Seras had witnessed today that madness of mutated corruption with his own eyes... trying to take away his life in order to create another monstrosity out of him. His resolve to fight that darkness was now greater than ever before.

"Seras! You are back! Your collar! Why are you a corporal now? Is everything ok with your hand canon?" Ladia's voice sounded genuinely relieved to see her former student hadn't been terminated yet. "Got promoted instead of executed. I guess it was my lucky day". The new corporal pronounced the words while demonstrating the full functionality of his hand canon arming it and disarming it quickly to show Ladia the extent of the repair. It certainly showed now an increase in reaction time that was easy to perceive with the naked eye. "I had an encounter with a corrupted operative from a special unit. I got promoted for blasting him before he managed to convert me". Seras pronounced the words putting some extra effort into trying to sound more business-like than usual. Whenever he was near Ladia he felt the need to prove himself to her for some reason. It could have been because of the time she spent training him, but there was something more to it... That girl made him be a better version of himself whenever they were together in battle. It was as if being in her presence heightened his senses and made him braver than he would normally be, breaking the limits the universe had set for him. That girl inspired him to thrive.

"Glad to see you are back in shape, kid". Lieutenant Jeqq pronounced the words accompanied by a military assistant that made sure to check the automated process of bringing Seras back to the unit had been done properly. It wasn't uncommon for evaluators to disdain bureaucratic procedures to the point of leaving them incomplete sometimes if more urgent matters required their attention.

"Yes Sir. Ready for service". Seras felt mildly annoyed by the absence of surprise in his Lieutenant's expression after seeing his new rank as corporal. "You know? We would have missed you down here if you had been..." The officer's sentence wasn't halted by anything awkward or sentimental, but by a general alarm that resonated through their communicators at the same time, indicating the presence of a new threat: "This is your general speaking. All available regiments go immediately to sector M3B. Maximum priority".

The way until reaching the assigned destination was tense and silent. The transport ship made regular noises that followed a determined pattern easy to recognize after a while. A maximum priority call meant an impending battle that would surpass any other encounter they may have had in the past. It was the first time such an order had been issued in living memory and even the most experienced members of the regiment 407 felt lost without any point of reference. "Listen up! This battle will be hard. We are instructed to use concentrated fire. If anyone gets corrupted, shoot them before they convert. Expect heavy casualties... It has been an honor to fight with you all". Lieutenant Jeqq's ominous silence after such a brief speech was the final sign for most to understand that they were unlikely to survive this mission. Most of the officers around were resolute, while at the same time asking themselves what type of terrible threat might have motivated such an alert.

"Seras, remember to roll and move positions after a few shots to make it difficult for the enemies to..." Ladia's explanation was interrupted by an unusual gesture. Seras took her hand and sighed deeply. "Ladia... I never got the chance to thank you for everything you have done for me. I know I haven't always been the easiest student but I..." An impact in the haul of the transport ship welcomed the 407 to the battlefield. With the round compact thrusters at the front of the ship damaged, the emergency stabilizers got activated on the sides to grant the troops more time to exit the vehicle. The deployment gates opened and as the ship prepared for an emergency landing, dozens of defense troops began to pour out of the vehicle hovering towards a vast group of corrupted chaos forces.

Unlike in past encounters, the enemy was this time well organized and their numbers were so vast that the scene defied all logic. Left and right officers could be seen enquiring through their communicators how was this scenario even possible. Corruption was supposed to be easy to identify since they moved in secrecy most of the time. The moment a deranged agent took too many risks by trying to convert someone openly in plain sight, the most likely result was a blast of hand canon to the face. Yet here they stood. Thousands of corrupted enemies ready to cause as much damage as possible to destroy a world they considered unjust and cruel for not allowing them the chance to be who they wanted to be. The established order that provided that world with prosperity was also seen as a prison for those who decided to follow their own way. Was it really fair to be eliminated if you couldn't perform a certain function in that society? For many living there became a cruel predicament once a problem threatened to render them useless. What some saw as mutated chaos, they saw it as freedom to be different.

The first exchange of shots favored the defense forces, but the enemies kept coming from all sides to reinforce their fallen comrades.

 "How could we have been so blind? This concentration of corrupt forces should have been spotted weeks ago. How can this be happening?" Lieutenant Jeqq seemed to be more worried about the lack of intel than about the vast number of enemies gathering in front of him. "Well... Lieutenant... Perhaps what you call chaos some of us call freedom, and perhaps the dream of freedom has infiltrated more units than you can imagine..." A quick shot from the side perforated the armor of one of Jeqq's assistants. Ladia's hand canon had been the first one to take the shot before the corrupted assistant could have caused more damage. Two other soldiers and a sergeant wearing protective equipment analyzed the body searching for tentacles and mutations that didn't take long to find.

Shots kept being fired at a rate that made it impossible to waste too much time in anything other than firing back.

"We need to report this immediately", said the Sergeant analyzing the body. "The communication systems in the area have been damaged. We need to reach the emergency beacon to send a signal. For The Goddess, we need to request massive analysis for mutation immediately. All units could be compromised! Trust no one who hasn't been analyzed. Shoot anyone who refuses the analysis!" Lieutenant Jeqq gave his orders and opened his jacket ready for inspection. One by one all the members of the 407 were tested and only two more soldiers had to be terminated, but the danger still remained for other units, and the forces of chaos kept attacking amidst the confusion, causing considerable casualties.

"We are losing too many soldiers! This is madness! Cover that right flank! We need to reach the emergency beacon whatever the cost!" As soon as Lieutenant Jeqq finished pronouncing those words, three shots coming from different angles of the battlefield perforated the chest plates of his armor. His death was unceremoniously followed by an automatic change of command where another lieutenant added the squadron to his current one decimated by enemy fire.

"He was a good leader. We will win this battle without him but for his honor. Direct all fire to that right flank! We will create a safe passage there!" The new lieutenant hadn't even bothered to introduce himself. His words towards his predecessor followed a cold protocol that disregarded anything unrelated to the mission at hand. Dying in service of The Goddess was not perceived as honorable if the mission wasn't accomplished, so the ultimate honor and value of Jeqq's sacrifice would have to be measured once the battle had finished.

The elements of chaos kept increasing their numbers, but gradually losing momentum and troops due to the combined efforts of the different regiments and their advanced weaponry. Chaos had a fundamental weakness: the markers were similar for all their members. The process of mutation occurred from one element to the next, so there was always a common trace that could be calibrated to adjust the weapon systems and minimize collateral damages in a battle.

"Let's move! We are almost there. Keep firing as you advance! The four of you, go deliver this message through the beacon! The rest of you, cover them!" The new lieutenant rubbed Seras the wrong way. Most of his orders were given as if he were speaking to fresh recruits. It was the most basic protocol to move while shooting. What other option was there? To casually stroll around without shooting back at the enemy didn't really seem like a good alternative plan. In any case the advance was slow and painful and the soldiers covering the rear took most of the heavy punishments.

"We are almost there! You! Take the message to the beacon, the three of us will cover you!" Ladia gave the message to one of the new soldiers and instructed Seras and the other one to shoot in all directions. Sadly, the cover provided by three hand canons was far from enough for such circumstances. Taking into account that this particular type of enemy was not prone to fear getting shot, a whole company wouldn't have provided enough cover. In their feeble minds twisted by chaos they were liberating their world from tyranny... and fighting for freedom against a dictatorial power established hundreds of generations ago. The only viable alternative for Ladia and Seras would have been to shoot each and every enemy before they noticed what they were trying to do, but with fewer numbers than those required for such a tactic, witnessing the death of the soldier carrying the message became inevitable and expected.

"I have an idea... This is not going to end well for us. Ladia.... I never told you that.... I think I love you. You make me a better version of myself and... I hope we can meet again in the next generations of The Goddess". After those brief clumsy words unable to convey much of what Seras was feeling at the moment, he took off his hand canon, set it to overload mode, and threw it at the enemies providing enough of an explosion to grant him a few seconds of much needed confusion and surprise to grab the message and introduce it in the beacon. He could have ducked for cover in one of the glistening red mounds next to him, but instead he hugged the beacon's console protecting it with his body to make sure the message was delivered. Two shots ended the life of the brave corporal that day as he heard his beloved Ladia shouting that she loved him too with tears falling down her pure innocent face. None of the soldiers in the 407 could have made a bigger display of emotion than those two corporals. Hardened by battle, loyal till the end, and blindly devoted to The Goddess. They could still show the ability to feel.

Ladia was severely injured seconds after eliminating three more enemies. Her wounds were taking her life slowly enough for her to watch the answer to the message. Central command had displayed their angels of death. Operatives far bigger than the regular defense forces arrived from the air causing havoc everywhere they went. Their orders were simple: to encapsulate the mutated elements of chaos in such a way that they couldn't spread their filth beyond that perimeter. Slowly but with an unbreakable power of will they created an outer prison to contain the enemies to the point of no escape.

When the fight was done and the dust had settled, chaos had been contained in a way that few other regiments had witnessed before, and never at such a massive scale. The bodies of their dead piling up on top of the ones still alive. What happened after that was a source of legends written for generations upon generations in that land. The red skies opened, the fabric of existence itself was separated in two, and a massive metallic frame appeared in the middle of the battlefield, removing the last trace of contained chaos from their world in a matter of hours; taking the filth beyond the limits of their own reality. One by one all the soldiers and operatives witnessing that miracle raised their weapons and cheered unanimously: "For The Goddess!"

Oblivious to the massive battle that had just taken place, a young girl waking up from surgery began making sense of the words she heard. "Allison... Allison... Can you hear me? It's Dr. Monroe speaking. Everything has gone well. The tumors turned out to be benign after all. This is very good news. How do you feel? It will still be a while before your head stops spinning. We are going to move you to a room after you rest a bit, ok?"

"Yes, I... I feel very tired. Is this normal?" Asked the girl. "Yes, I am afraid your immune system must have been working overtime in the last days. The fever is relatively stable, but if it doesn't go down in a few hours call the nurses, ok? We are all glad you are ok".

Billions of unheard voices rejoiced that day, and all of them repeated one and same message: "For The Goddess!"

INTERDIMENSIONAL GUARDIAN

The rain hit Jerome's bike as he was making his way through the traffic. At times like this he had the impulse to second-guess the decision of selling his car to do some more sport. It was one of those things that felt good only when you receive the cash, and then in nice sunny days. When the storm hits you hard as you come back from work, and the raincoat stops performing its basic duties, biking starts feeling like a mistake. Luckily he would soon be home enjoying a bowl of chow mein soup and a juicy steak with mashed potatoes and sauce. He would be cooking it all himself. Finishing a cooking course for singles at a local school had made him extremely cocky about his skills, so even if the sauce took him as much time to prepare as the rest of the dishes, making it himself added an additional feeling of accomplishment.

"Damn son! That raincoat of yours ain't doing a thing!" Mr. Diller always had it easy to spot Jerome from his newsstand with those white and red lights blinking intermittently on the bike. "Have you tried adjusting the laces inside? I had no idea half of my jackets had those until my wife told me! On our second date... That woman was gold. God rest her soul..." The old man always got emotional whenever he remembered something connected to his wife. Every time Mr. Diller told Jerome that he was the only black guy in Bedford Town who knew how to cook Asian food, Jerome felt the need to answer back something about Mr. Diller being the only black guy in Bedford Town with a Vietnamese wife, but he stopped himself every time. Jerome had a big mouth, but he was also sane enough not to cross that line since that wonderful woman had recently passed away.

The two men would often look for any excuse to have a lengthy conversation about whatever topic was in the news that day. Anything would do... They would start with the local news or the latest political scandal and gradually move further and further away until the topic had something to do with galaxies, mysterious monsters in Latin American jungles, or the implications of time traveling. Mr. Diller was like one of those chocolates that had a regular wrapping but was hiding some unusual interesting flavor. Jerome was sure that many of the regulars buying stuff at his newsstand had no idea that the man was a perfectly calibrated thinking machine that would make jokes about big breasts and follow them with something like: "You know Jerome? If a machine could travel in time it would need to be anchored to the floor in some way... If you left it floating, the planet would keep moving through space and you would reach your destination but the planet would be somewhere else across the galaxy... Do you know what I mean? Uh! Look at them titties! Where do you think she is from? A fine young lady! She looks Dominican or something..."

"I think I have seen her near my architecture studio", said Jerome.

"You know? Most people would just say they saw the girl near the job".

"Yeah, I know... It took me a while to graduate so I try to make it count mentioning the thing as much as I can. Architecture... Architect... Studio of..."

"Yeah, yeah... Anyway, what have you been working on lately?"

"Some renovation plans for a couple of office buildings. Nothing exciting. They want to install solar panels on the roof too, and no expert seems able to make them understand that sun is necessary for those things to work at least a bit".

"It sounds as if they just want to tick a box or two to appear sustainable, green, and all that stuff". Mr. Diller had just verbalized Jerome's impressions at his last meeting with the clients.

"Well... that's it for me today. I gotta go make some dinner. Always a pleasure to talk with you Mr. Diller!"

"Take care J!"

Jerome parked his bike and used the small lantern in his keyring to aim with the key a bit better. Those little gestures of efficiency were always appreciated by his clients because they made it look less likely for a building to fall if the guy in charge of the project worries about spare pens, little lanterns, and tying his shoes with a double knot.

A dozen lifetimes would have not prepared Jerome for the scene he saw inside his kitchen. A random guy cooking dinner and a little blonde girl sitting on a chair and staring down visibly embarrassed. The guy had an average height, white, a little trimmed moustache, and was wearing a shirt with rolled-up sleeves, a very thin tie, and a vest. Everything about his clothes screamed something along the lines of: "I have picked these clothes at random from a 1920's golf brochure".

"What the fuck do you think you are doing in my kitchen?" Jerome remembered about the little girl and immediately felt irrationally guilty for using that type of language, despite finding an intruder inside his own home.

"Oh! Mr. Atkins! I beg your forgiveness. Please do excuse my manners. Your daughter was hungry and I thought you wouldn't mind me cooking once I had explained you the full situation".

"My what? My daughter? Are you insane? Dude... step away from the fires and start talking". Jerome eyed the cooking knives on the kitchen table, that were still closer to the intruder than to himself even after making the guy step away.

"Mr. Atkins... I assure you, we mean you no harm, but if you feel safer holding one of those knives, by all means..." The man moved the knife set closer to Jerome with two fingers in a slow mocking gesture and continued talking. "You seem to have a technical profile in this reality as well, so I am going to assume that you are familiar with theories about time and space being one single concept and all that..." The man perceived the uneasiness in Jerome's movements and decided to go for the shortcut version of that whole conversation. "Here... this is a message from yourself in the reality we come from, to yourself in this reality... Do you think you can handle this? Do you need me to speak slower perhaps?"

"Look, I don't know what your plan is entering my home with this bullsh... this nonsense about space and realities. I think this is one of those times when calling the cops is in order..." Jerome went for his phone but the intruder was faster to activate the hologram. A familiar yet unknown voice began to speak to him as the kitchen covered in multidimensional images of constructions too bizarre for them to be a product of someone's imagination:

"My dear Jerome. This must all be very difficult for you to grasp at this point. I am sorry for disturbing your life like this, but please be sure I would have never thought about this extreme measure if there was any other option available. I am you from a different reality. You could say it is your past, but in a different world of humans that would probably look like the future to you. This reincarnation comes later in your timeline after the current life you are living so we have all been dead for millions of years in this planet and... Oh, something tells me I am doing as bad a job explaining the situation as Xur". The intruder pointed at himself and smiled: "That's my name by the way... I was rude enough not to introduce myself, and... to trespass and start cooking without permission... I am starting to see things from your perspective Mr. Atkins. I should have handled this differently...heh... sorry".

The man passed two of his fingers over the hologram device and the recording continued: "There are different realities for humans to evolve and develop. Think of it as the soul choosing different environments to experience complex situations and feelings... Does it sound reasonable to you with your current knowledge?"

Jerome protested: "Hey! I am not stupid, ok? Keep playing that thing... I mean, even if this turns out to be a joke or something, the hologram is quite cool... This is anything but boring. You got my full attention... Keep playing it... Let's see where this goes".

The hologram resumed, and the kitchen surfaces once again showed the alien scenery and the pale blond man speaking with a sound that seemed to come from all directions: "Daug wal naum shiraf eresen..." "Oh! Sorry, I forgot to put it in your language..." Xur smiled at the little girl with complicity and adjusted the message.

"Wait... Yeah, the hologram can be adjusted, fine... I'll buy that, but how is it that you are speaking perfect English if you come from a different dimension and all that?" Jerome finished his question with the air of a detective who has managed to land an incriminatory blow that would solve the case.

"Do you really want to know that now? Really? There is a different version of you from another dimension explaining you the secrets of the universe and you want to know about language modules? Ok then... Have it your way my good sir. Linguistic abilities are all over the brain. They are connected and influenced by many different processes. Developing the technology to use a foreign language as well as your own without learning it first would require a wide range of cerebral connections, whereas simply translating what you express in your own language with an automatic updated database that can synchronize your lips before you speak is relatively simple. If you pay attention you will see slight twitches and vibrations in some words when we speak too fast and... I'm sorry, am I boring you Mr. Atkins? I seem to recall you were the one who requested this very explanation".

"Yeah, I know... Sorry. It's just that... jut saying -translation technology- would have been enough. I didn't really need all that stuff about lips twitching, but ok... Can we go on with the hologram?" Jerome had gone from feeling uneasy to feeling interested in what these strangers had to show him. The young architect was composing a puzzle with different pieces, and seeing that his question about the language thing didn't get him anywhere, he quickly lost interest.

"In this reality you have a daughter and two wives but it would be hard to explain all the intricacies of our society right now. Suffice it to say that I love both my wives very much, as well as our daughter Lish. There has been a conflicting reading about her soul needs and this has created a problem between those who think that there may not be mistakes in a soul path big enough to justify a change of dimension millions of years into the future, and those like me who want to make sure Lish and others like her can reach their full potential, even if that means sending her there with you. I understand all these concepts poured at once may be overwhelming considering your current state of mind, but to simplify this: If our daughter doesn't experience life with you, she will waste her time in another reincarnation further on..." Xur paused the hologram. "You look puzzled, is there anything I can help you understand?"

"Yeah.... yeah.... right.... A few things. So... There is a group of people from that dimension interested in getting the little girl back, right? So when they come here with their futuristic guns... What then? And if that world is gone why don't they all travel through other dimensions? And why can't the father come too? Or you... like... Why exactly do you need me in the picture if you can show her around?" Jerome thought it might be best to give the strange visitor some time to answer.

"First of all, nobody is going to harm you or Lish. Violence against little girls is not something very popular in our world. They would just take her away and that's it. You are in no danger Mr. Atkins. Nobody is going to come to your dimension bearing futuristic weapons of any kind. Her father and I have no business being here, since we would spoil her life experience simply by our presence. Keep in mind that in your culture protecting life is important, but in our culture making sure that everyone fulfills the life experiences they are alive for is also essential. Nothing bad will happen to the girl, there will be no laser shootings in the middle of New York, and nobody in our world has any interest in wandering around alien worlds that could be fatal at any moment, spoiling their current reincarnation and making it start all over again with similar circumstances". Xur finished his speech with a remark. "You know what I should be doing now? I should be bathing with my girl in a violet pond with cascades creating amazing memories and learning the true meaning of bonding with a loved one... Do you think being in your kitchen in Bedford Town brings me close or far away from my life goals for this cycle?"

"Err... Yeah, that thing you said sounds legit I guess... But this is all very weird. I am open-minded and what not, but this is all freakishly weird, really... What am I supposed to do with the little girl? How much time does she have to stay here?" Asked Jerome.

"Just a few days. Try to avoid anyone looking out of place and time. She shouldn't return before it is time. Here, have some gold coins from your world to purchase things and services without troubles". Xur put three bags of gold coins on the kitchen table and Jerome examined the contents of one of them. "Gold sovereigns from 1912? What the hell am I supposed to do with these?"

Xur looked at the man confused. "What do you mean? Did gold lose its value since that year? The data I had showed that currencies could not always be exchanged easily, but gold should be accepted in plenty of different places..."

After a few more questions and playing some parts of the hologram for a second time, Jerome began to realize that everything he had witnessed that night was too bizarre for any other explanation than what he had been told being the truth. He started to think about the implications of refusing to help these people. He couldn't completely understand the full extent of what he had been asked to do, but he prided himself in being smart, and open to new concepts. Against all odds, he quickly came to terms with the idea of having a guest from another dimension with him for a few days, even if the idea of this little girl being his daughter sounded crazy to him.

"Look... whatever... I can take care of this little girl if it's so important to you and all that, but how will she come back after doing whatever she has to do?"

"Excellent question Mr. Atkins. We will take her back when the time is right, until then we have created a few decoys and plans to slow the authorities down. If there is anything else you need to know, you can ask Lish. She is a bit shy, but a very intelligent girl. I hope you two get along well, and thank you once again for your hospitality towards us here tonight". Xur put his fingertips together and joined his elbows twice, activating some device or technology that opened a portal where indeed a pond with a violet liquid could be seen at a distance.

"Oooook then... Well, it's just you and me kid. Are you still hungry? Do you want some dessert?"

"Yes please. Thank you" Lish smiled following every movement Jerome made around the kitchen as if she were looking at the most interesting show in the world.

"How is this gonna be? Do you know what you have to do or do we just go around sightseeing and stuff?" Jerome served two bowls of ice cream and made gestures with his hand to show Lish how the spoon was supposed to be used.

"Thank you. I know how to use a spoon because before coming here my other dad and uncle Xur made me learn. Thank you for the ice cream".

"You are welcome... Look, no need to thank me every time for everything... Here it's kinda hm... implied... I mean... you can thank me if you want, but damn! You don't need to do it all the time. One more thing... It's gonna look strange if you call me -dad- while you are here... Everyone around here knows I am single and... well, our skin tones are different and it could freak people out. Do you know what I mean? Like: -Hey Jerome, I didn't know you had a six-year-old white daughter! Way to keep a secret man!".

"Ok". The little girl smiled at Jerome and started to explain him how she would love to see planet Earth with all the animals, the forests, the oceans, and what not. She became a bit disappointed to learn the amount of time it would take to move from one ocean to the next with the limited technology of this particular reality, but she found comfort in the second ball of ice cream. Learning everything about the planet would certainly be something difficult to manage in a few days.

"What exactly do you have to do here?" Asked Jerome. "I don't know... learn about this place I guess, so that I don't have to come here 140 years..." Lish kept devouring the ice cream as Jerome raised an eyebrow. "What do you mean 140 years? How much do you people usually live?" "Hmm... I don't know. One of my grandmas lived a lot! More than 170 years for sure! But the other five are still alive"

As the little girl focused on the task of finishing the ice cream, Jerome rubbed one of his eyes with the palm of his hand while trying not to think too much about how messed up it would be to have six different grandmothers at the same time all telling you how skinny you look and offering you dish after dish.

"Can I play with lights before going to the mattress?" Lish looked up with the hope of getting an affirmative answer. "What do you mean by -playing with lights-? What mattress? Did you mean the bed?" he asked. "Yes, the bed. Is it on the floor like on the wooden huts from the Earth videos?" She took a circle from her pocket and lights of different colors began to move in the air while she arranged them into different figures of unknown creatures. "Erm... The mattress here goes inside a bed frame and you are elevated a bit from the floor... This is not a tropical beach where you can just throw a mattress on the floor and..." Jerome realized his tone had begun to sound annoyed and impatient towards her innocent questions. The little girl's world was as foreign to him as planet Earth was to her. "Hum... what I mean is that you probably saw images and things of our planet but in different places we do different things so... here we sleep with some distance from the floor" "Why?" asked Lish still painting in the air with those projected lights. "I don't really know why... I guess the floor is cold, or maybe too hard to put a mattress there just like that. I never asked myself that question... Can I try those things?" Jerome sat down next to her and quickly got the hang of it, but had no idea how to let one light go to pick another color, so he just painted in a consecutive line trying to hide that fact as part of his chromatic plan.

"Ok, time for bed. Tomorrow I will call my job and let them know I came up with the flu or something. Did you bring a toothbrush by any chance? I may have a spare one in the bathroom". Without saying a word, the little girl opened her mouth showing her teeth and did some gesture with her hand. The bracelet she was carrying released a small flying robot that entered her mouth and applied light beams of two different colors for a few seconds. "I need to spit now..." With his eyes widely open, Jerome pointed at the kitchen sink. Lish struggled to reach it, but managed to rinse her mouth with a glass of water.

"This is your bed. You have water bottles in that cabinet. If you wake up before I do, don't touch anything dangerous, ok? Nothing electrical, no leaving the house, and all that stuff. Are we clear?" "Yes. Thank you" Lish smiled apologetically, unsure if her presence there was wanted or not.

"Gnight Lish. This is as strange for you as it is for me. I don't totally understand this situation, but make yourself at home, ok?" Lish nodded with a broad smile on her face. It was almost as if Jerome had read her mind.

It took him hours to fall asleep thinking about all the interactions of the evening and remembering over and over picking up on small details that had passed unnoticed. For example the attitude of the guy cooking dinner... It's one thing to watch videos or visual materials about Earth, but it didn't seem as if that guy were using those cooking utensils for the first time. Could it be that these people are advanced enough to have flying robots for dental hygiene but still cook using pans and pots? What could this mean? Jerome twisted and turned a bit in bed and finally fell asleep as his frown disappeared from his face.

When he woke up the next morning, he found Lish wearing a dress that seemed to have come from a 1950s movie. She was sitting on the sofa with her legs crossed and drawing shapes and things with lights just like the night before. When she saw Jerome, she went up to hug him. The surprise on his face was quickly gone, and he hugged her back with one arm while laughing nervously. "Hey, hey! Are you hungry? I'm gonna make us some waffles, and a couple of sandwiches to take with us. Would you like to see something in particular?" "I don't know... Something fun?" "Ok then! Listen... You've got to remember how strange it would look if you call me dad in public for the people that..." Jerome stopped himself and reconsidered his words. "You know what? Change of plans... You are adopted. Yeah! If anyone asks I got you from an orphanage in Ukraine, alright?" Lish smiled and then remembered about something. She started to make some movements over her wristband and she answered something in perfect Ukrainian. "Oh! Damn! That thing can make you speak any language in the world, right? Do you know how much time we waste here learning them one by one?

Damn...What do you want with your waffles? Do you know about caramel?"

After a breakfast filled with more questions by both sides they left the house and began to walk till the train station. Along the way a few people were surprised to see a blonde girl in a 50s dress looking at everything in amazement, touching the lamp posts, and stopping to admire every shop window and every animal she encountered.

"Two tickets please. Grand Central". The old clerk had been recently hired thanks to a popular and curious trend that made people more likely to use transports and services if a human was there to offer the service rather than a ticket machine. "Shouldn't you be in school now?" said the clerk jokingly. "I come from Ukraine. School hasn't started for me yet" Lish smiled aware of her childish charm and its usefulness to avoid further questions. "Oh! Ukraine! Beautiful country!" The clerk had pronounced the words not having the slightest idea where to locate Ukraine on a map, but the gesture was appreciated anyway. Jerome winked at her for her performance.

The train ride was full of questions, asked mostly in whispers and with Jerome finding out more and more about his other self and the culture in which he had developed. Some of the technologies were wildly original, but unfortunately Lish was too young to explain them with the level of detail that an architect required. "Wait, so this place you visited with your family... had a circular tube that would make you freefall for minutes? How? The base of the tube must have some mechanism to avoid collisions and such, right?" "I don't know... You have to wear a special suit and they take you... I didn't fly alone... They didn't let you the first times" Jerome was fascinated listening to all the stories and learning more about Lish's world.

New York was a place of wonder for Lish. All those buildings, the shops, the traffic. Everything was primitive and at the same time functional for her. They entered Central Park and her questions began once again. "Why are all the windows in a square shape?"

Asked Lish. "What do you mean? What shape should they have?" "Well... different ones? Like... Nobody wants a house with round windows here? I saw videos of houses after the cataclysm and..." Lish's bracelet began to create a vibration and pulses of orange light and she went silent.

"Wait! What cataclysm? What are you talking about?" Jerome realized that if this child was from a civilization long gone, and she had watched videos of his time, there was nothing to stop her from watching videos of future decades. He realized there and then that Lish knew about Earth's future. "Lish... You gotta tell me. What cataclysm is that? When does it happen?" "Well... It's too early but... Hmm... Soon... One of those mountains with smoke is going to go off and..." "Mountain with smoke? A volcano? When?"

Lish smiled and gave him her hand. "Please! Come with us. It's not your time yet. We came here for you!". Jerome began to make more sense of everything that had happened so far. He fell to his knees and began to cry. "You are not here to learn anything about this world... Are you? You... you came here to save me from that volcano... But why? Why me?"

Lish smiled, with a mixture of shame for her lies, and joy for finally being able to tell Jerome the truth. Xur was faster than her though. Appearing at the distance waving, when he was close enough to Jerome he offered his hand to pull him up. "Mr. Atkins... I am sorry for our little deception. When Lish learned that one of her dad's reincarnations was going to perish in this planet, she asked if we could help. We thought you would be more receptive to the idea of helping a little girl than to the idea of leaving your planet after simply hearing our stories. Your conversations with Lish and your limited contact with our technology and way of living have made the process easier and less stressful for you. It's still very difficult... But imagine how much harder it would have been without this little adaptation process".

Jerome breathed deeply, and exhaled trying to contain his tears. "What volcano will it be? There must be something I can do! Why saving only me? Can we save more people? Can we save them all?"

"Oh, no Mr. Atkins... I am afraid I haven't expressed your current circumstances well. We can take you with us because you have a connection with our culture through your other reincarnation. Most of the people sharing this planet with you are doing so at an initial stage. Their first steps at this level of spiritual development would not benefit from coming with us, even if we were allowed to take them. Likewise, some of them are too advanced... just here to collect a few particular life experiences as babies or toddlers, and then ready to go to the light, and to their next life adventure". Xur smiled condescendingly, but his expression quickly filled with empathy... "If it makes you feel any better, Mr. Diller and you are also friends in other lives... But I think this is all quite confusing as it is without telling you more about all that".

"What about my dad? My friends... How much time do I have?" Asked Jerome with a sad expression on his face. "Two more days". "Are you sure I can't save any of them?" "Yes Mr. Atkins... It is hard seeing loved ones go, but you must accept they have already fulfilled their paths in this reality. Their passing will not be painful. I promise you that much".

"What about the reconstruction? Lish mentioned something about..." "Yes, indeed, there will be a reconstruction, but not with the humans currently living here. The planet will be suitable for human life after some time, but this generation of humans will be long gone". Xur smiled politely trying to imagine how difficult all this must sound for Jerome.

"Two days... just two days... I would like to say my goodbyes. Is that possible?" "Yes Mr. Atkins, but please don't mention the cataclysm. It would unsettle them, and it may alter their state of mind... It could make their transition process more stressful than it should be".

Jerome understood the explanations provided to him, but he couldn't stop feeling guilty for the people he left behind. "Are you sure we can't save anyone else?" He asked. "Mr. Atkins... Look at it this way: You wouldn't be saving them, you would be preventing them from going on with their paths. Your case is a statistical anomaly. Only a handful of humans will be relocated to other planets due to their special circumstances". "How is my life there gonna be? What am I going to do? Do you guys need architects?"

The three of them started to walk through Central Park and Lish held Jerome's hand. "Don't worry dad... You will never be alone there! You have us!" Jerome turned his head and smiled at her. "Will you teach me how to paint with those lights of yours?"

The little girl nodded and asked to see the ocean while enjoying an ice cream.

STRANDED BY DESTINY

He got up from the floor as if waking up from a dream. His body felt weird, and he didn't recognize the landscape around him at first.

"Get up! We don't pay you to lay on the floor!" The taskmaster's whip showed its full length before being charged for the first of several lashes to come.

The kid, 16 years at most, instinctively dodged the blow, and went towards his attacker with a rage unseen by anyone around him up till that point. He jumped in the air using the momentum of his left leg going back to hit with his elbow breaking the nose of the taskmaster and falling with one knee on the floor. He looked around trying to identify possible threats and realized the nearest guy with another whip was too far away to notice anything of what had just happened.

-What have you done child! You have doomed us all!- An old lady battered more by the exhausting field work than by the years addressed Kaolan with horror in her eyes.
-I did what needed to be done. Where am I? How did I get here? I want answers!- His words came out with a disdain that surprised even himself.
-Have you lost your mind Kaolan? Where did you learn to fight like that? Your mother and I never taught you any of....- The words of the man speaking were interrupted by the cold stare of a kid who judged him a stranger.
-My mother is dead; so is my father. I have no idea who any of these people are but I want answers and I want them now!-
-Kao, what are you saying? Come back to your senses... We have been years working on these fields. Remember? Is this a heatstroke? Have you lost your memory?- Said a young man about the same age as him.
-Hm... Apparently I have. Look... I may not remember who I am or how I got here... but I can tell you I am not one of you. This place is vaguely familiar, but those two for sure don't feel like my parents, and the rest of you don't even look familiar at all.

The people around him had the shock of their lives upon hearing those words uttered without the slightest semblance of hesitation. They started murmuring among themselves while Kaolan, realizing the taskmaster was recovering his consciousness, picked the belt tying his humble brown robe, and started strangling the man, whose departure from this world was as shocking as unexpected.

-You... you.... killed one of the guardians... You murdered him... Do you have any idea what the punishment for that is? They will kill all of us! They will...- The utterances of the man were quickly answered in a brief and sharp way.
-This doesn't look like a life worth living. Death would come as a liberation for most of you. You work on these fields like slaves while men on horses beat you? Is that it? And you fear death? Why? What do you have to lose? What is so great about your lives that you need to protect it with submission?

Kaolan didn't wait for an answer. He took the taskmaster's
yellow vest, his dark green hat of a triangular shape, and he
folded his own robe tying it up on the waist to imitate the lower
part of the taskmaster's uniform. He mounted the horse and
went straight for the other man in charge of a second group of
workers. He didn't even need the protection of that disguise,
since the man was too complacent about his own safety, and too
uninterested in the movements of the other taskmasters to
notice the horse that slowly approached him at a steady pace.
Kaolan threw the whip towards the left side of the horse,
startling the man, and immediately grabbed him by the other
side in a semi-circular movement that enveloped him and took
him to the floor. The movements where precise and had the
desired effect of using the victim to absorb the blow of the fall.
He pounded on the man a few times and began his interrogation.

-How many are left?
-Left of what? Wh... Who are you? I will have you torn by horses
for this!
-Not the answer I was looking for.

He punched him another time and got up while the man
struggled to incorporate himself at the same time he cleaned
some blood off his mouth.

-Bad news. I am looking around and I see only that small wooden
outpost. How many men could fit inside that tower? Two more?
Maybe three? Never mind... Oh? You keep patting your right
pocket... Are you looking for your knife? How rude of me to take
it away while you fell. It's only fair that I give it back I guess.

The man tried to protect himself with his hands but the knife
was thrown with a strange deliberate effect that made it hard to
predict where it would land. Direct to the throat.

-I guess I could fight the other slavers, but I rather burn the
tower from the base and watch them get consumed by the
flames. Press the wound with your palm... It would be a shame if
you missed the show.

In the blink of an eye, right after pronouncing that sentence, Kaolan found himself inside a cave, lit by a few torches, where a beautiful girl with long black hair sat relaxed trying to peel a fruit with her delicate hands.

-Oh! You are back! Did you have another one of those episodes of yours?- Her smile was like a soothing medicine for a tired soul.
-I... I am sorry... I don't really know who you are, but you look familiar. Please don't feel insulted.
-Hih! Insulted? My future husband has dimensional jumps! It's an everlasting source of entertainment hearing about your adventures! Tell me... where did you go this time?
-I don't know... It was like another land where I had to kill some slaveholders.
-Oh my! Were you in danger? Please tell me you were ok there. Are you hurt?- She held his arm as he was sitting down near her ready to grab a piece of the fruit she had peeled.
-No, I didn't feel in any real danger but... I didn't know why I was there and... although this is nice... I don't really know who you are or why am I here.
-Don't worry about that. It takes you a few hours to regain your memory after one of your adventures.- She kissed him gently on the lips and hugged him in a way that would make sure both of them would end up falling softly over the big hides making the floor of the cave comfortable. Kaolan kissed her with all the passion he could muster, and began making love to his future wife feeling blessed to be with her.

-I am glad that I look familiar to you this time. I wish we could stay like this forever...
-What do you mean? Do I perceive sadness in your words?
-When will your memory come back? It's too painful to explain you this time after time. Sooner or later there will be war in the land and... I don't want to be away from you. Please... give up your responsibilities... Isn't this better? Isn't love better than war?
-Well... It's hard to argue with that. I wouldn't really care if my

memory never came back. Being here with you is the closest to paradise I can imagine. What's your name?

Kaolan kissed her neck and caressed her soft skin while thinking about how lucky he was to be desired by such a beautiful creature. When he was about to kiss her lips, he closed his eyes, but when he opened them again there was no trace of the beautiful girl. Instead, in front of him there was a courtroom and a weeping man on his knees pleading for his life.

-Sir? Your honor? Are you ready to listen to the defendant's testimony?- A serious man with a perfectly trimmed moustache waited impatiently for an answer looking as if he had asked that same question a few times already.
-What? A trial? How?
-Your honor... Are you ok? Do you wish to call for a recess?- His tone sounded as polite as annoyed at the prospect of a delay.
-Yes... I... A recess.
-The trial will be resumed after the recess! His honor will hear the final testimony of the defendant and pass a sentence after the recess! Long live the Empire!

Kaolan got up from the chair, left the room and began to make sense of this new scenario. The girl had mentioned something about leaving the present moment to fight in different situations, but she had said nothing about trials. As he walked down the big corridors of that strange building mixture of temple and courthouse, he realized the people around him were wearing clothes in completely different styles and materials from the ones he had seen before. Visibly confused, he started to ponder his situation.

-Wait... How can I remember the slavers and the cave but nothing before that? Why are those memories with me but everything else seems forgotten? Unless... Is any of this even real? None of this makes any sense...

He sat down on a strange ivory-looking chair with a semi-circular shape and began to feel trapped and scared about his situation. Where had the girl gone? Why was he in this courthouse? He breathed deeply a few times and got up just in time to be taken to the courtroom by another one of the men sitting at the table with him.

-Everybody sit down! The testimony hearing will begin!
-Your honor... You must believe me... I am innocent. There isn't a single proof of any of the accusations. The witnesses all belong to the Shawkas and their testimony is not valid. They would say anything to protect their Lord, the real killer! He couldn't bear the thought of her daughter and I being together so he killed her and framed me! You have heard my witnesses... I was far away when the events happened, and I loved that girl more than anything in the world...

The man sitting next to Kaolan leaned over to whisper something in his ear: -Your honor... remember everything at stake here. Don't let the words of this man distract you from the greater good... from the big picture. What is a man's life compared to avoiding a war where thousands would die? Think of those lives...

Kaolan looked around him and felt a shiver.

-You know what? This doesn't even make sense. Everything seems tailored and artificial. Who would speak like that? Exposing all that information in such a brief period of time... Why? Unless you are perfectly aware that I just appeared here recently and I have no idea about what's going on. I mean... why would you explain me that thing about the war at this point of the trial?
-Your honor, I don't know what to say.
-You know what? It feels like I am the one on trial. If this man is innocent I am not going to convict him just to avoid a war... Let those soldiers do their duty and die if they must! They will die with their honor intact knowing they haven't been spared thanks to the blood of an innocent dying in their place! You there! I declare you innocent. You may go.

Kaolan saw the people in the room move slightly slower than they should, as if their movements had been expanded a fraction of a second, and distinctly got a concept in his head: "This simulation is over".

In the next blink of his eyes, he found himself floating in a big round room where the walls expanded and contracted slightly, producing a variety of colors with particular soothing tones that made him feel safe and relaxed. Three figures appeared in front of him. Two of them stayed hidden in a weird artificial mental blur that was difficult for him to understand. It was as if he knew those figures were there, but his brain refused to focus on them or translate their presence into valid information. It felt as watching something in the dark without being able to identify the shape, with the small difference that the light in the place should have allowed for those shapes to make sense. The central figure was a creature with a round elongated head that stared at Kaolan with two main eyes that were dark and large, and 3 smaller eyes in the upper corners of the main ones that didn't articulate or move at all. The creature had a round mouth without teeth on a dark grey skin and communicated directly with Kaolan's mind without producing any sounds. The young man felt an instant wave of empathy and goodness emanating from that being in front of him.

-Kaolan. You are safe here. There is no need to be scared here with us. If you please, would you give me your consent to explain you why you have failed your test?

The young man felt even more relaxed and noticed for the first time that he was missing his human body. He was only a consciousness with a self-image that did not match his current shape. He moved his hand and realized the three fingers in front of his face had five phalanxes, so he could move and bend them in ways that felt unfamiliar.

-Where am I? Am I free to go?- Asked the young man without moving his mouth.
-Yes, nothing restrains you here. You are free to leave if you wish. Is that what you desire to do, or do you want answers from me?

Kaolan immediately realized that leaving without any idea of what was happening was probably the worst thing he could do considering the circumstances, but he was reassured about his safety there after being told that he could leave at any time.

-What test have I failed? What was the purpose of it?
-Remember. The memories will start to come back to you little by little. You chose to test your impulses as a different life form devoid of your current knowledge. Does this concept sound familiar to you so far?

The young man began to receive flashes of feelings and situations that weren't accompanied by visual information. He had direct feelings of having embarked voluntarily in all those experiences but without those sensations being attached to the distinct memory of a conversation or anything of that sort. His way of experiencing reality was now different, and he acquired new emotions and ways to process them.

-What was this test? Is this my true form?
-All your shapes are your true form. All your names are your true name. You wanted to try your primary impulses under primitive circumstances. The recreation of that world was a test for your choices.
-So none of it was real?- He began to get new flashes and sensations and answered his own question: -Wait, yes... Everything was designed, but the experiences were real. I remember now. When will I remember everything?
-If I may be bold enough to say this myself, with my explanations you will reach those memories more efficiently. You have to abandon some knowledge and personal essence before venturing in a primal experience like this. Do you wish me to explain you why you failed or do you already possess those memories by now?

Kaolan stopped to reconsider. He understood that the answers he sought were already inside him, and he just had to access them naturally as he had always done before his primal experience.

-I failed the first part because I didn't save any of the slaves suffering injustices there. I killed those guards instead of simply

restraining them, and I was going to burn that primitive
construction without even knowing who was inside or if they
were guilty or innocent of any crimes.
-I see the memories are appearing faster and faster. Why did you
fail the second part?
-I don't know yet... The flashes are not coming to me.
-If I may suggest something... There is no need to be hasty. You
have as much time as you need.
-The girl. The human female. I chose her over my responsibilities
in that primitive conflict she was mentioning, right? Is that it?
-Right again. You didn't display the primitive impulse of helping
others without establishing them as part of your life experience
first. Choosing pleasure over duty would have caused people to
suffer and die without your help.
-Why did I fail the third part then?
-You didn't. Your primal instincts were right in that case. But
justice alone doesn't make a good spiritual base if you are unable
to apply it in general and without attachment or involvement. If
you do what is just only when you are in the position of a judge,
your fairness is impaired and limited.
-Yes, I remember those things now. My fair actions can't be
based only on acquired wisdom. I should be able to display
justice and fairness as a primitive instinct too.
-Excellent. Would you like to try again, this time allowing for a
basic ethical compass?
-I would like that very much. I thank you for your help brother
Gha'lung. I hope to be worthy of the trial this next time.
-It is an honor for me to help a future brother Decider reach his
full potential. Let's go once again then, shall we? With your
permission.

The round room began to change colors and the three beings
became perfectly clear for Kaolan's mind. They were familiar to
him in a friendly way, and the new flashes coming to his brain
connected his current real form with his memories of past
simulated experiences. To become a brother Decider would mean
to apply flawless ethics to improve the development of society in
this and other worlds, so relying on wisdom alone would be

dangerous. He needed to train over and over until he could decide between right and wrong beyond his intellectual limitations. He focused on the light patterns changing the colors and as he placed an image of his home world in his mind, he prepared for a new test.

Kaolan opened his eyes and found himself on a fishing ship, unable to tell how he had arrived there. He could listen to an argument taking place about the execution of some prisoner...

THE RISE OF A HUMAN EMPIRE

Chapter 1

The two children ran to the training grounds as they did almost every afternoon to see the knights with the power armors. Fei and Alec used the way there to see who could run faster, and strange as it may sound it would always be a close call to determine who arrived first to the stone separation on the slope that connected with the training quarters of the local units. The knights had a wide variety of trainings, but the most spectacular ones were those where a squad fought another one using all the available strategies at their disposal.

A squad was formed by a knight with a power armor and four support soldiers with regular ones that acted as a single elite unit with devastating efficiency. Alec touched the stone separation with his right hand and the smirk on his face crowned him as the champion of the race for that day. After a couple of days losing to Fei, he felt like he needed that victory. It was never pleasant for a boy to lose in a race to a girl over and over, so some measure of balance had been achieved that day. He sat down on a section of the stone, cleaned the place next to him with his sleeve and comically invited his friend to sit down. Fei put herself in position while the squads prepared their armors and offered Alec some homemade squares with a spongy texture and a honey-like taste.

-Do you think Captain Alden will be in one of the squads today?- Asked Alec.
-Nya! I don't think so. His father has probably sent him to one of the outer planets so he can go up the ranks without too much danger. A few more missions and he could be Star Captain. Imagine! A guy from here! From our own city!
-There have been a lot of exploration missions this season. It must be so cool to travel around space. I would love to be a soldier so damn much...
-Yeah Alec, I know... You tell me that almost every day. I get the idea. But you know that the chances of...

Fei's explanation was cut abruptly by the sound of the power armors being activated and the soldiers' armors being pressurized and ready for combat. The distinctive hissing of the air flowing was the signal that the whole training combat was about to happen. The lieutenant with golden stripes on his shoulder pads positioned two of his support soldiers in the air above one of the opposing squad's soldiers, and instructed the other two to stall the rest of the opponents with smoke and light shots. In turn, the ensign with green stripes, despite being inexperienced and having a lower rank, went directly to attack the two soldiers causing the smoke while instructing his own four soldiers to defend against the enemy squad flying to the same spot so singling one of them out would prove impossible.

With the first blow he had almost caught one of his objectives off-guard, but he soon showed his true intentions when he fired a restraint mechanism from his wrist to catch the legs of the second soldier. Breaking those restraints wouldn't be difficult even for a soldier's armor and their limited capabilities, but it would take him some precious seconds in which the opposing team would be down one man. Instead of finishing the other soldier in that wing of the field, he immediately flew to encounter his opposing lieutenant, who did the same knowing that his only chance to win this exercise now was to defeat that ensign before the rival soldiers overpowered his own on the right wing. His attacking moves were powerful, but the ensign just defended and blocked with his forearms, until he saw the chance to sweep the lieutenant's front foot after covering his vision with the palm of his right hand. The destabilized lieutenant fell to the floor, but instead of finishing him, risking a counterattack on the floor, where he wasn't particularly fluent yet, he ran and jumped towards the second soldier on that wing, throwing him to the ground and then pushing him out of the battleground's limits using the element of surprise.

His four men had overpowered their target by now and deactivated his helmet with a twist, meaning that if the battle had been real, the man would have a broken neck or a depressurized helmet in an alien planet without the right pressure or breathing conditions for him to survive much longer.

The young ensign sent his four men to finish the last remaining soldier quickly, which they did by grabbing his legs and arms in a coordinated tactic, and then pushing him out of the battleground. In a bold move, the soldier had grabbed one of them before falling, so his defeat had brought some benefit to his team by dragging one of the rivaling soldiers along with him out of the field. The lieutenant flew towards his restrained soldier to free him faster, but the ensign proved his cunning preparations to be nothing but a trap. He instructed his three soldiers to use their smoke shots now all at once, making the left wing of the battlefield a complicated area for seeing anything. The lieutenant, unable to clearly see his soldier, charged head on towards the ensign, but protected by most of his squad, the combat was lost beforehand. A few good attacks, some good defenses, but in the end the lieutenant ended once again with his back on the floor and his arms restrained by two of the soldiers. His helmet was depressurized slowly and in a theatrical way to let him know that time wouldn't have saved him anyway in that situation.

Fei and Alec both cheered at the end of the training exercise, visibly impressed by all the strategy and planning that had made such a victory possible. For them it was always a fantastic show despite witnessing such exercises almost every afternoon after their classes at the academy.

-Why can't they give power armors to the soldiers as well? I mean... Why making them fight with worse armors if they have the technology to give them better ones?- Asked Fei with a tone too serious for her young age.
-Dunno... It's probably expensive to build those. The costs of the military would go through the roof if they gave everyone top equipment. Besides, what would be the point in getting to be an armored knight if any soldier could have what you are wearing?- Alec realized he had made two very good points and he leaned back a bit with a proud smile on his face. Forgetting the measurements of the stone elevation where they sat, he fell back landing on the grass with one foot stuck in a round bush.
-Ah hah hah hah! Clumsy! Clumsy! You areeee so clumsyyyy!!!- Fei could hardly contain her laughter, and for a second she was at a risk of falling herself but from the other side of the stone separation.
-Ouch! Not funny... My ankle... It hurts... I think it might be broken.
-Wait, don't move. I am going to call some soldier for help.

Before Fei could even stand up to run towards the soldiers, two of them from different squads came to check on the boy. The sheer reaction speed of those soldiers was enough testament to their skills. Seconds after Alec had fallen, they were already flying towards his position.

-Everything alright here, kids?- Said one of the soldiers.
-I... I think I have broken my ankle. Sorry for interrupting your...
-Nonsense! It's no interruption at all. It's more like a well-earned rest.- Said the second soldier with a smile.
-You two are big fans, aren't you? We have noticed you watching our trainings a few times- The first one of the soldiers had taken his emergency medical kit and was trying to distract Alec from the pain.
-Wait Harth! He might be allergic to light pulses. What's your

name, kid? Have you ever been checked with pulses before?
-Well... yes, when I was a baby but I don't remember. Oh! Alec.
My name is Alec, sir, and she is Fei.
-Pleased to meet you both Alec and Fei. I am Harth and this
elegant fellow wearing a uniform from the Dark Squad is Jurik.
Well, if you have already been checked before, it means you are
certainly not allergic. In any case, don't stare at the light, ok? It's
too strong without protection. You too Fei, you can see the
reflection on Alec's skin, but don't look at my wrist during the
process. Clear? I am going to put this metal blanket under your
leg. Don't move.

Both children nodded as the soldier prepared his medical gear to
examine Alec's leg. If everything was right, the light would not
be received by the other end of the mechanism in any strange
way. If there was a fracture or a broken surface, the light would
be able to pass through it, indicating the precise nature of the
wound.

-Good news. It's just a sprain. You will be up and running in no
time. Jurik can fly you home if you wish. I will inform our
commanding officers so they don't think we are deserting or
something, hah?- The soldier's comment made both children
laugh.
-What's the name of that ensign? He is very good!- Said Fei.
-My commanding officer? His name is Tayak. He is extremely
cunning!

After being delivered home by the soldier, Alec had to suffer a bit
of scolding from his mom, while his dad tried to calm her down
saying the usual things in these cases: "kids need to play", "we
all fell from places when we were children", etc. The statistical
relevance of those assertions didn't seem to make Alec's mom
totally calm about the incident, but she stopped her scolding long
enough to thank Jurik for having brought her son to the house. If
that woman's opinion of the soldiers was good before, now she
was in awe of their kindness.

The next day, Fei visited Alec to let him copy her notes for a couple of classes, and couldn't stop praising the soldiers.

-And the way they flew... it was so cool! And Hath was so handsome! Do you think he is single? I wonder what type of girl would be attractive for a guy like him...
-Harth... His name was Harth... If you are planning to go on and on about how handsome he was, the least you need to do is to remember his name correctly.
-Uh! Feeling a bit grumpy today, aren't you? Or perhaps you are jealous... Could that be it?- Fei put her hands on her hips and waited for a reaction knowing Alec felt really uncomfortable in these situations.
-Me? Jealous? Why would I be? You are too young for that soldier anyway... Besides why would I be jealous? Pfff....
-Well... I will grow up, you know? I don't plan on being 11 years old forever!
-Yeah, yeah... I am sure he will wait for you and then you can both have a family and what not... Can you pass me the other roll? I still need to copy that one.
-Aha... The roll, sure... Anyway it's just a few exercises and a few notes on history. It starts from the red mark, before that you should have everything already.
-Oh Fei! Will you stay for dinner? I have to head now to the headquarters for a mission, but my wife will be happy if you stay. You know how much she likes drawing with you and playing instruments!- Alec's dad was one of those people who seem to be always in a good mood. He only got angry if a transport made him late for an appointment or something like that. Keilan, the man with the perennial smile on his face.
-Oh! I would love to! But my parents have guests and they need me to be there and in my best behavior... Ugh!

Fei pouted involuntarily as if her parents' expectations posed an unbearable burden to endure. Once Keilan left, she began asking loads of questions about the mission, the role of an administrator in those trips outside the solar system, and anything else that popped in her mind. Her curiosity was insatiable.

-Yeah, and then they land in formation, but my dad and the other technicians stay inside the ship so they rarely see any action. In the last mission they didn't even set foot on that planet- Said Alec with a thoughtful expression.
-Oh! And why don't they visit asteroids? Why only planets or big moons?
-Well... I am no expert but the suits and the ship can adjust for the... thing... the... gravitational something. The... ugh, it's difficult to explain, ok? If they land on a planet they can walk around and if they land in a small asteroid they could still float away cause they are... smaller or... You know what? I will ask my dad when he is back, but the asteroids are smaller than the satellites so I know that has something to do with it. They need special modules and stuff for those.
-Oh, ok... They can't just walk on an asteroid, right? Heh! Got it. I gotta go now. I'll drop by tomorrow again. Take care clumsy!- She took one piece of fruit from a bowl on the table and smiled at Alec.

Chapter 2

The reconnaissance ship was about to enter the orbit of planet Xalke, in the neighboring solar system of Kifias-4. The numbers attached to each new solar system discovered were merely an indication about the possibilities they offered. A class 4 solar system wasn't a waste of time, but it was certainly nothing to write home about. The different planets and moons there were mostly used as an amusement or an adventure for the explorers after a mission had finished. If the environment was suitable enough, they could play sports, project audiovisual entertainment over vast lands, and explore the territory for new species of life forms.

-Sorry to hear that... When will your boy's foot be alright?- Asked one of the officers in the administration deck of the ship.
-Just a few days and he will be as good as new, heh! That will teach him to be more careful the next time!- Said Keilan while adjusting some travel logs.
-Poor kid! Missing the knights' trainings for days must be tough.

Is he still going on and on about entering the military service? Wouldn't he prefer to be an administrator like his dad? Or a scientist? Scientists get armors too sometimes!
-Oh! As obsessed as ever! For a kid his age I guess what we do here must sound very boring. Nothing beats the adventure of a soldier's life. I can't compete with my stories: "Oh son! I know you watched flying soldiers in combat doing crazy stuff, but I was adjusting the ship's logs to make sure our landing was safe... that's cool too, right?"

The administrative officers and a couple of scientists began to laugh; a laughter that got interrupted by the holographic display of the ship's commander on the ceiling of their room: -Gentlemen, ladies, the probes have located the missing ship badly damaged and there seems to be signs of violence. Gear up for defense and make sure we are ready.

-What enemies could we have in this sector? It's not such a new discovery. This doesn't make any sense- Said one of the scientists with a troubled expression.
-Someone managed to damage a military ship. Never a good sign. Let's hope the probes are wrong- Said another one of the administrators.

Before the ship touched land, the defense probes were already in position, and the three knights on board took their soldiers out to secure the perimeter in a formation of triangle sweeps. The ship landed and connected to the emergency system of the damaged vessel as the knight squads approached the area.

-For everything that's holy! This is a massacre! Why? Who would do such a thing?- Captain Glein made no effort to hide his shock from his men. He firmly believed a good officer draws power from his honesty, so his reactions were always genuine.
-Sir, we have found two more bodies near that lake. Coordinates K82130, V91377.
-Squad 2, escort the scientists for an analysis. Squad 3, scan from the air for signs of life beyond our perimeter.-Ordered

Captain Glein to the two lieutenant knights forming the rest of his team.

The scene they witnessed inside the ship was bizarre beyond reasoning. None of the men had their armors equipped, and all of them showed signs of having been brutally murdered with basic weapons. Near the lake, the captain saw two naked men, one body had three rudimentary spears traversing it, while the other had two and a wound to the head made by a series of attacks performed with a blunt object.

-Administrators, please include the untimely death of Captain Alden in the priority logs. We assume command of his vessel and mission from this point onward. Notify the governor that his son is dead, along with the rest of his crew. Scientists, please make a full analysis of the perimeter and study each of the corpses in detail. I suspect things are not what they appear to be.

They set the artificial lights to float on the perimeter and once the orbs where in place, they prepared to study the data collected from the ship, and from the medical chambers performing the autopsies. After a few hours Captain Glein gave surprising new instructions: -Input poison and advanced weaponry as parameters for the second autopsy.

-Sir, may I ask what theory are you working on?- Enquired one of the lieutenants.
-I saw burnt flesh next to the other wounds. I also suspect one of the men near the lake showed signs of poisoning. The spears and the other injuries don't have much coagulation. If they had pierced those men when they were still alive there would be puddles of blood instead of just a few stains. Their hearts weren't beating at the time of those attacks. This is all very suspicious.
-Captain Glein, one of the analysis on the blue fruits hanging from those trees show signs of poison. Does this confirm your theory?
-Are you telling me they ate unknown poisonous fruits without analyzing them first like you just did? Like the protocols demand?- Answered the captain.

-No sir... What I am saying is... It's very strange. Those fruits are not supposed to be poisonous. The logs in their ship show several other visits to this planet and plenty of testing for the environment. It seems that they came here to have some fun after their missions were over. At least seven other times, sir. They knew the area well, apparently.
-So the poisoning of the fruits was intentional. A trap? By whom?

The captain inspected the ship's logs for a few minutes but suddenly the alarms north of the perimeter activated, initiating a tactical response from two of the squads.

-Sir, we appear to have 29 humanoid creatures carrying spears. The preliminary analysis shows they are wearing masks and green paint. Do we engage the enemy, sir?
-No, don't initiate any attack, lieutenant. We must tread carefully. This is all too strange. Don't make any mistakes. Are there voice logs in the damaged ship? I will go to speak with them myself.
-I am afraid the data collection for voice analysis is insufficient to have a meaningful conversation with those creatures, captain. I doubt you can understand more than 20% of what they are saying, and they won't understand you either as you know- Said one of the scientists from the ship through the communication system located in the helmet of the armor. The lady was entirely right. Trying to figure out a language purely through computational force required a vast sample material that hadn't been collected.
-None of the protocols have been followed by that ship while staying on this planet and I want to know why. Soldiers, diamond formation at a distance. I need answers from those creatures- The soldiers organized themselves in a way in which they could cover the captain without being considered part of a conversation party. A man alone addressing a crowd was always less threatening.

Captain Glein flew slowly towards the group but made the last approach walking calmly and showing his palms with his arms at the level of his waist. It was a clear universal way to show he was not hiding any weapon. The technicalities of this logic made no sense considering the offense capabilities of any regular armor, but for individuals that were holding wooden spears, the fact that the captain wasn't carrying a spear himself was clearly comforting.

-Captain's log. The creatures didn't show surprise or fear watching me fly towards them. It could be a sign that they have seen flying armors before. Removing my helmet's mask and leaving it on auto-engage.
-Careful captain... They could turn violent at any moment- Said one of his soldiers.
-I know, Ermin. Even if they attack I don't want you to do anything. Those spears pose no threat to our armors. I repeat: stand down. Do not engage unless they have more dangerous weapons.

As soon as the captain was in range, the local tribesmen began throwing their spears at him. The helmet's mask went back on, and the kinetic deflectors softened the blows of the projectiles to the point where the impacts were not even interrupting the motions of the captain while advancing towards them. He marked four targets for extraction and issued the order to his soldiers. The formation flew on top of the group and covered them with smoke. The selected targets where constraint in an instant and carried to the ship while the captain calmly flew away from the disoriented group of humanoid aliens covered in smoke.

-Activate the ship's non-lethal defenses. Sound, light, and propellers. Under the powers invested in me as an officer of the empire, I hereby declare these creatures as prisoners of our vessel for attacking me with lethal intent. Their language is to be studied before a military interrogation can occur. Disinfect them and scan for known strains of viruses and biological threats before placing them in a confined area.

The orders of the captain where specific and precise. The members of his crew knew that he had a plan, but they were not confident enough to ask him directly about it for fear of interfering with his thinking process. They didn't have to wait much for answers. In times of peace the captain's log is made free-to-access material for any and all members on board a vessel.

-Captain's log. After being attacked without provocation, I am within my right to consider the identified subjects as hostile forces. They have been taken as prisoners to be released after a successful interrogation has taken place. My initial suspicions have to do with foul play. None of the crew members of Captain Alden's ship were wearing their armors, and they ate fruits poisoned on purpose with a substance to be determined. I suspect these men felt safe and comfortable in this planet, and used it as a relaxing spot after their missions.-

With the limited knowledge of the prisoners' language, they were instructed by the language program of the ship to name a series of objects that would appear in different images. The process would take some time, but it would increase the percentage of linguistic knowledge available for the interrogation. The method was purposefully designed in a simple way. Cooperation created a peaceful environment and calming conditions, resistance to comply with the linguistic acquisition protocol would create sounds at a variety of frequencies that would bother the subject in a non-lethal way and without permanent damage. After the process had produced enough material, the subjects were left to interact with each other to learn more about intonation, mannerisms, and non-verbal cues.

As the prisoners completed the linguistic protocol and the rest of the crew slept, Administrator Keilan could only think about his wife and the recovering leg of his son. He was only distracted from his thoughts when a group of those local individuals came too close to the ship and received disorienting light flashes or the same calibrated sounds that created discomfort for the prisoners inside, upon refusing to cooperate. Only once during the night were the propellers activated in a defensive mode to throw back a couple of females that had covered their eyes and ears and were advancing towards the ship more than necessary. They would have never been able to damage the entry doors with their limited technology, but the defense protocol had to be followed anyway to avoid penalties and negative outcomes once the ship was back home and the travel logs were checked.

The results provided by the language program were then calibrated between the answers given by the different individuals, and their form of communication could already be decoded at more than 70%. This gave a better chance of getting the results Captain Glein was looking for. Lacking sleep, and afraid for what may happen, the five individuals sat on the floor. The captain sat down next to them to create a positive environment for communication.

-Surprised, captain? Once we removed their masks they turned out to be humanoids. Not entirely human, but quite similar to us in structure. They seem to have evolved from a similar species, but not too much as you can see. The hair on their bodies is real, but the green tone of their skin is just a rudimentary pigment extracted from local plants.
-Thank you Dr. Lemara. That will be all. Please complete the analysis of the damaged ship and its logs. I want to know what caused the tragedy. Certainly it wasn't these creatures with their pointy sticks.
-Certainly not, captain. I will have it all ready in no time.
-Thank you doctor. Let's begin, shall we? Activate translation in 3,2,1... "Why did you kill the members of the other ship?" "Why did you attack me yesterday?" "Have you had any other ships visiting you?"
-Captain, I am afraid the system doesn't have the word "member". I will adjust it to "people from the ship".- Said one of the administrators.

The responses did not disappoint. Captain Glein was forming an accurate theory in his mind, and these creatures were confirming parts of it.

-Captain, they claim that they didn't kill the crew of that ship. They were used to their presence in the area, and they had grown fond of the exchanges of items that the ships bring. They attacked you thinking you were going to kill them for the death of the crew members apparently. Very typical of these primitive cultures... They feel threatened and they attack first to have an advantage. Don't ask them for much logic... There are members of their tribe still trying to reach our ship after hours of failed attempts.

-The protocols establish that no exchanges of items may occur with the local population of a class 4 system.

-Yes captain, the protocols also establish that one should always analyze the food in external planets before consumption, as well as armored soldiers on guard even if most of the crew is swimming naked in some lake. There should always be a security perimeter and as you can see none of these procedures were followed.

-What about the ships? Insist on that point- Said the captain.

-One of the females claims that two other ships have been visiting. The two ships together. "Friend ships" is what the translation says. Did we have two ships in this sector at the same time?

-No. We didn't. Try to get me a description for those two ships and the people inside them. I want the rest of you to go through the logs and security footage of the ship, soldiers included. We have been attacked and poisoned and I want to know why and by who. Release the prisoners after the interrogation is complete.

-Yes captain!

The day passed with frantic efforts to collect the valuable clues that would help clarify this mystery. The idea in everyone's mind had quickly shifted from an act of war to a convoluted plan that went beyond basic aggression and made them pieces in an intricate game that they had been underestimated for. After a long meditation session in his personal cabin, Captain Glein's mind gained the clarity to make the right choice.

-Change of directives. Prepare the damaged ship. We are taking it with us. Are the bodies of those men all on board?- The captain decided to abandon rhetorical questions and accessed the ship's logs himself, satisfied to know everything was ready for a departure.

-Captain, may I ask what you have in mind?- Asked one of his lieutenants.

-Yes. We are about to be attacked, because we didn't take the bait.

-Attacked? What bait?

-Think about it lieutenant. Two more ships have been seen here by the locals. Advanced synthetic poisons in the fruits our soldiers would eat like they had done in their previous visits, and a neatly prepared welcoming party with the same spears piercing the corpses of our men. We are being baited into attacking the local humanoids.

-The captain is correct at least about the spears. The locals have traded them for other items when the other ships came. For them all the ships look the same, but from their descriptions they could belong to the Faksi or the Netauh.

-Or they could have been disguised and prepared to look like those ships. Only one way to find out who is behind this. We have released the prisoners instead of slaughtering them as a revenge, and we have prepared the damaged ship for transport and thorough examination at home. If your plan to start a conflict had failed, and your targets had obtained information that could discover your plot, what would be the only possibility left for you?

-Oh... Stars be praised... Prepare for an imminent attack... Correct, captain? We should leave this planet as fast as we can...

-Not yet. How would we know who's behind this if we don't allow them to reveal themselves? Prepare a fake departure and maintain all defensive systems ready.

-Captain, we don't know how many they are, but they know we have three squads, 15 operative armors, if they have been observing us as you suspect. I have an idea you might like.-Dr. Lemara grinned.

She explained her plan in detail and everyone seemed to like it, despite the dangers it would entail. Captain Glein protested about the idea, even though he recognized it was an optimal move directly out of the ingenious mind of the doctor.

-I can't ask the administrators and scientists to assume such combat risks. It is entirely voluntary. Does any of you volunteer for this plan?

All the crew members stepped forward with their right fist in a diagonal position touching their left shoulders. It was the traditional way to indicate they all agreed to participate in that mission as volunteers.

Chapter 3

The ship slowly began to display signs of initiating the departure, but all the procedures were done a bit slower than usual to give the enemy time to prepare an attack. They didn't disappoint. Not long after the propellers had been positioned for takeoff, 5 assault squads appeared in the horizon flying at a considerable speed. A total of 30 armored men, since their squad formations had 5 soldiers plus an officer commanding them. Carrying portable distance weapons that were a mixture of projectiles with an energy field around them, the idea was to penetrate the haul of the ship as it had no reason to have the defensive systems prepared during a takeoff maneuver. Unfortunately for them, the ship had no intention of going anywhere, and activated the defenses and shields. The ship's weapons targeted one of the enemy squads with full force. It wouldn't destroy their armors or finish them in any way, but it would stall them and balance the battlefield a bit more since they wouldn't be able to fly. If they wanted to make use of their kinetic deflectors they would need to be on land and allow the armor to correct their movements. Doing the same in mid-air would be impossible for them.

The enemies landed in front of the ship's three defensive squads commanded by Captain Glein. The enemy officer, seeing that one of his squads was having troubles, initiated a conversation with the idea of wasting a bit of time to allow them to rejoin the group.

-Itano, itano... hassi urukme lau neifter shain...
-Wait, it will be hard to understand you if you don't let me activate the translation beacon first. If you are Natauh or Faksi we should have your languages correctly mapped- The captain made a signal with two fingers and a floating ball positioned itself in each side of the battlefield.
-Well, well... Seems nothing has happened according to the plan. If only you had killed that local Shahiri tribe as you were supposed to. What kind of captain sees his fellow soldiers killed with spears and doesn't seek revenge when given the chance?
-Shahiri. Include that name in the logs for future reference. Squads 4 and 5, engage- Captain Glein ignored the enemy officer's words as if they were nothing but a nuisance at that moment.
-Squads 4 and 5? Impossible! That type of ship carries only three squads. We have only seen three squads while you were here... Why would you carry more and keep them hidden? It's highly irregular...
-It is. Unless we were informed of your plans beforehand. That's why I didn't attack those Shahiri humanoids, that's why I have kept hidden forces, and that's why the ship's defenses were activated. We have infiltrated your ranks. It seems that some of your men are actually our men- The captain's bluff was blunt, but believable enough to spark a shadow of doubt in the mind of the enemy officer. Indeed too many things in his plan had failed, and treason seemed highly plausible at this point.
-Wait. There is no need for a massacre to happen here. If we disengage and we leave, there will be no blood spilled. What do you think, captain? Your soldiers would also be spared their wounds.
-Squad 6, engage.
-Wait... 6 squads? Please, wait... From an officer to another officer. There must be something else than bloodshed here for us.
-There is only surrender or death for you here- The captain

sounded confident and pretended to be impatient to finish the enemy forces as fast as possible.
-We surrender. Disengage your squads please.
-Take off your helmets and move forward- Said the captain.

The enemies did as instructed while an increasing number of armors flew around them, five squads in total. The sixth group of armors remained near the ship in battle formation, still and ready for action... or so it seemed to the enemies.

-Wait... The colors... The sixth squad has the same color on their shoulders and helmets than this other squad that... Your colors never repeat in a ship's formation. What is this? How can this be? It's a trick! They took the armors from the other ship! Put the helmets back on!
-Too late for that I'm afraid. Activate the ship's non-lethal defenses. Protocol 9.

Just as it had happened with the local Shahiri humanoids that tried to attack the ship, the disturbing lights and mixed frequency sounds incapacitated the enemies without the protection of their helmets. The three real squads had no troubles restraining them, including the officers. When their slowest squad arrived to the battlefield, although they had their helmets still on unaware of the unfolding of the last events, they showed no fighting spirit. Their fellow soldiers and officers had been captured, and trying to flee didn't seem like a possible option with the ship's defenses locked on them. Unable to fly, they surrendered as well.

-Take them on board. Good job everyone. I wonder how it must feel to know you were overpowered by administrators and scientists who barely know how to fly one of these armors.
-Hey! I may not be an expert, but I used a couple of these in the academy- Said Keilan swollen with the pride of his first military victory in a battlefield.
-I am sure you did, Administrator Keilan. And I must say that I am very proud of you all.

The ship left the planet with their new guests secured. The journey back home allowed them to extract information from the prisoners and from the extensive damaged ship's logs, but in doing so Captain Glein felt more uneasy about the whole situation. The enemy armors and their way of behaving had the clear trademark of the Netauh colonies. The different human colonies present in that sector of the galaxy had come to control different solar systems. Theoretically speaking there should be enough planets and satellites to keep all those factions and civilizations busy for thousands of years discovering them all. Unfortunately human nature is such that no matter how much territory they control, as soon as they come into contact with another group of humans they feel the need to eliminate the possible threat, or conquer it by force. After all, an empire that is already built is a more valuable prize than an empty rock floating in space. The Netauh were no exception to this logic. If this episode had been orchestrated by their rulers, it meant they were paying too much attention to other inhabited solar systems and could be more interested in conquer than in exploration.

-Maximum priority! Start sending all the collected data as an emergency signal. Inform the local headquarters, and send encrypted copies of everything you can manage to upload to the Administrative Guild, to the Science Guild... I want all this to reach as many people as possible! Everybody, put on your armors! Activate the defenses. Administrators and scientists as well. We are still at risk of an attack! Interrogate the prisoners again by any means necessary! I want to know if they were acting alone or if there are more ships after us!

Captain Glein realized it was naive of him to think the attacks on that planet were the actions of some rogue group of soldiers instead of a coordinated effort to create a conflict that would offer an excuse to start a war, and perhaps even an alliance against their home solar system. The boldness of the poisonings, the desire to frame the Shahiri humanoids to get them killed, and the perfect excuse to claim that an atrocious crime had been committed against an innocent rudimentary civilization. Now that the plan had failed, it was unlikely that the Netauh would allow those prisoners to act as witnesses that would dismantle that and other possible ploys.

-Everybody! Equip your armors or the ones you used during the battle. Administrators and scientists as well! We are still at risk of being attacked. Prepare the shields and the decoys, and for all the stars in the sky keep sending copies of those damn logs!- Nobody had ever seen the captain so nervous, which gave them a sense of impending danger that made them hurry up with the tasks.
-Don't worry so much captain. You have us here as prisoners. If there was any chance of being attacked by Netauh ships I would be the first one to tell you. I have no interest in dying here due to friendly fire. I am no martyr. Calm down...- The enemy captain sat down calmly in his containment cell as members of the crew frantically moved around him.

-Hey you! What's your name? You fly well for an administrator- Said one of the girls in the confinement cells.
-My name is Keilan, and I have a wife at home and very little time to waste with you right now. Excuse me.
-My name is Arisha, and I am bored in this cell. Perhaps later we can exchange some stories? It would be good for you to start learning things about the empire that will soon conquer your system.
-Aha... and I suppose you know a lot about all that?- Said Keilan.
-More than you can imagine. I am an intelligence officer. And I have a secret to share with you. Would you be interested? Something I learned while analyzing your ship with our scanners. I bet you would love to know... otherwise you will all be dead soon.
-Oh, lucky me! A secret... Do tell.-Keilan mocked the girl while organizing some logs to input through the console to his right.
-This ship is in danger, and I don't want to die here. Promise me you will take me to a safety pod... And I will tell you what I found.

The girl's revelations proved to be a surprise for most but not for Dr. Lemara. Her suspicions had been confirmed following a series of recent events.
-So... The rumors were true...- Dr. Lemara left the confinement area and approached the captain with a look of horror in her eyes.

-Captain, the encrypted transmission has been rejected by the Science Guild and by the local authority... after being received by the military headquarters. I have tried to send the messages again but they are rejecting them on purpose. I don't expect you to believe what I am about to say to you right now but... I beg you to sabotage the emergency systems and evacuate the ship manually with the safety pods, or we will all be dead in minutes.

Captain Glein looked into Dr. Lemara's eyes and realized this woman was putting her career on the line with a request that was outrageous and bizarre considering her usual behavior. Against all logic, he granted her request and gave the order to evacuate the ship.

-What about us captain? You are responsible for the safety of your prisoners!- Said the enemy captain.
-The way I see it, if you wanted to be protected by military conventions you should have tried diplomacy instead of poisoning and murdering those unarmed men and women.- The cold tone of the captain reflected his hatred for those crimes. He muted the confinement cells, sedated the prisoners with the gas mechanism, and ordered his crew to board the safety pods immediately. The only available planet to land them was a desolate and barren place that would prove almost as unforgiving as the cold darkness of space.

From the safe distance of their pods, the members of the crew saw their ship get obliterated in a kind of explosion where the fire disappeared as soon as it came into contact with the vacuum of space.

-How did they do that? What hit the ship? Has anyone seen it? Where are the enemy ships?- Asked one of the lieutenants wearing his armor inside the pod.

-There are no enemy ships... Are there, doctor?- The voice of Captain Glein sounded through the communication system from another safety pod.

-No captain. I am afraid the explosion is not to be blamed on our enemies.- Said Dr. Lemara.

-Wh... What? What does that mean? Who else could have done that if not an enemy ship?- Asked the lieutenant visibly nervous.

-Control yourself, officer! Why don't you explain him the situation, doctor?

-I... Well... There has always been this rumor about the... The rumors claim there is a self-destruct mechanism for the ships we use outside our solar system.

-Allow me to correct you, doctor. A self-destruct mechanism would allow me, the captain of the ship, to destruct it. That's not what this is after all, is it?

-I know Glein, I mean... captain... I would have also been blown to pieces along with the rest of you. But why would they decide to kill us all?

-I don't know yet doctor, but you can be sure I will find out.- Answered the captain.

-How exactly? Looks like we will be stranded on that planet for a while.

-I have given my life to the service of the Empire just like all of you. That destruction order had to come from the top. Someone in the highest places of government has tried to eliminate us and I will make sure they pay for their crimes.- Captain Glein acquired a somber tone as his words resonated within the pod.

-Captain, if I may, I am afraid this goes deeper. If that sabotaging device could be found inside our ship, and they have a protocol for it, they might have destroyed more ships in the past years. Think about it... These atrocities go far within the leadership of the Empire.- Keilan pronounced the words and his mind immediately drifted towards his family. They would have no way of knowing what had happened to him for some time. What would life be for him without them? And for them living without any certainty.

In his home planet, there was a devastated child who received the news from Ensign Tayak that his father had died in action due to unknown circumstances. A child that had suddenly been forced to leave childhood behind as he accepted that life had dealt him a fatal blow, depriving him of his dad when he needed him the most.

-Alec, I know how you are feeling right now but you must remember you are not alone. You have your mother, your friends, and our whole society behind you.
-What I don't have is my father. Thank you sir, but how could you possibly know what I am feeling right now?- Alec tried to fight the tears that came to his eyes as he pronounced the words.
-You are speaking to an orphan. I lost my parents in an exploratory mission just like you. It was my first year in the military academy, just a year older than you are right now. I lost them both at the same time... I was also devastated. Feeling betrayed by life.
-How did you cope with the... the pain...
-I didn't. I train hard every day to be the best officer I can be.
-But what's the connection with...
-Knights with the rank of lieutenant can choose their own training missions. All sectors and all planets, including those forbidden by the directorate.
-What do you mean?
-I mean that as soon as I become a lieutenant I can investigate what happened to my parents. I would suggest you to do the same if you want some closure.
-I don't want closure... I want answers. Thank you Ensign Tayak, for sharing this with me.
-Anything you need, let me know, ok?

Alec Dagenshar thanked the ensign for showing him the way and promised himself then and there that he would find out the truth about what had happened to his father, but that... is a story for another time.

THE MAN WHO SAW THE OTHER WORLDS

The chubby tourist adjusted his backpack once more so the shoulder straps didn't have to hurt as much as the day before. Trying to save a few coins in his equipment had to be one of the worst ideas that had ever crossed his mind. He took a sip from his water bottle more as a mechanized process to stay hydrated than as a response to thirst. He had been told too many times about the possibility of having a heatstroke to ignore that scenario, and quite frankly the possibility of becoming a patient at one of those hospitals in Nepal made him quite nervous. Not because of some inherently negative opinion about them, but due to the fact that he had chosen to cut corners in his travel insurance as well. That was the type of traveler he was, one of those terrified by bureaucracy to the point of disregarding personal safety.

He began ascending the long way formed by a combination of flights of stairs and a tendency to overlook the comfort of those who wanted to approach the temple. It was a place clearly designed to discourage those outside from going up there, and those inside from having the temptation to mingle casually with the local population.

Out of breath and visibly exhausted, the overweight traveler adjusted the different straps that kept his belongings in place, and knocked on the door. He looked around in different directions as if trying to form a mental image of the place to draw it later. In those moments of silence where not even the sounds of his own footsteps could distract his mind, the thought that maybe he had lost his mind going to that forsaken place began to grow stronger. Suddenly, he was taken away from this dialogue with his inner voice by a strong and low sound of the thick wooden door being moved, and left ajar.

-Welcome traveler. What is it you seek?
-I... Yes, hi... My name is... George Keilnner, with a double N, I mean, it sounds the same. It's just for when you write it... not that you are going to write my name now... Excuse me, I am a bit

nervous. I tend to babble when I am... hm... nervous.
-You have time. Time to calm down, time to focus on your
thoughts.
-No... heh... that's the thing. I don't have much time, actually.
Erm... I am here because I was told in your hm... in your faith, in
your religion, I wouldn't like to offend you by using the wrong
words. I believe inclusivity is important when dealing with exotic
cultures and... oh God, not that your culture is exotic and mine is
the norm... That is not what I meant at all. I meant it is exotic to
me, since it's my first time here, sir... or madam, or any type of
way you prefer me to address you... I am fine with it, really...

The monk wearing a traditional brown tunic over a dark orange
vest with a soft collar, stared at the man not sure if his confusion
was entirely honest, or if part of it was an exaggerated attempt
to conform to some type of behavior entirely foreign to him and
his environment.

-I see. Well George, pleased to meet you. You can call me Zatoh
or brother Zatoh. As you prefer. May I ask what brings you to us?
-Yes, pleased to meet you too. I... it's difficult to explain. I am a
writer, you see? I am not very good at the trade, I mean, I am not
bad or anything, just... not spectacular and... Well, I went to a
seminar recently... for writers, you see? And, well I didn't learn
much there... at least not much about making my stories better
but... Well, there was a man there who was waiting for a... a
friend I think, or his boyfriend maybe... Which is beautiful
because I respect everyone's choices and... Anyway, this man was
a painter or an artist, like... a graphic artist and...

Mr. Keilnner had managed the impossible. The monk looked
visibly irritated due to a powerful combination of his chaotic
speech and his strange comments that complicated an already
monotonous discourse.

-George. What can we do for you here?
-Oh yes, I was getting there. I do have a habit of beating around
the bush; that I do! Well... This painter, he... talked about a
friend of his, also a painter who had a... how to call it? A period

in his life where he didn't have any inspiration and... well he was the one to mention this place and the thing you did for him... the... connection and...

-There are more temples like this, George- The monk had uttered that sentence unaware of the implications. The personality of that man in front of him was so annoying that his first impulse had been to send him to some other temple hundreds of kilometers away. He smiled politely and breathed heavily, trying to correct the tone of his statement with further explanations. - What I mean is that it is common for temples to help people, not only ours is happy to be helpful.

-Yes, I... I appreciate it, really. Well this artist he... apparently got some inspiration here from the... the connection... Do you call it like that? Oh... I wouldn't like to sound... I mean, I respect your beliefs and I was wondering if you could perhaps help me with...

-With what exactly? Are you also an artist, besides being a writer?

-Me? Oh, no... Just a writer. I was... well I was wondering if perhaps your connection with those other places could help me to... to get some ideas... I... don't really know what to write about anymore. I have lost my touch... Not that I am famous or anything... oh God, no... I am just average and unimportant, but... perhaps before I had more ideas to write about and recently I... well... I stare at the empty page and I don't know what to tell my readers. They aren't a lot, but... writing is everything I know how to do. I mean, I am not an expert or anything, but...

-Yes. I understood. Follow me.

-Oh, yes, thanks... heh...

Zatoh's voice showed a dislike for George's way of speaking, and for his overall personality, which far from being something usual or expected, was a rare feeling the monk hadn't experienced in years. George had an uncommon talent to be instantly disliked by truth-seeking monks in a secluded mountain.

-Wait here please.

Translated from Maithili
-Hey Zatoh! Who was at the door?
-Hi Sheng. A very weird foreign guy. He asked if I was a woman
or something else.
-Oh! Like the guys in the videos! Did he ask if you were a cat too?
Remember that girl? She wanted to be a cat... Hah!
-Yes... I remember her. Sometimes I think the walls of the
temple are not high enough.
-It will pass. Balance always returns. What does this man need?
-Inspiration. He is a writer who doesn't know what to write
about.
-Like a fisherman who doesn't know what to do with a rod...
-Yes. I couldn't have said it better myself. Do you think you can
help him out? I am busy helping brother Osho in the garden.
-I will do my best. What's his name?
-George Keilnar or something like that. I call him George.

Outside the wooden room, the chubby man swayed his body
slightly from side to side as he waited, and smiled to anyone he
crossed eyes with, as if wanting to let them know he was not a
threat or something like that. George's thoughts were tangled
and difficult to comprehend even when he was explaining them.

-George! Pleased to meet you! My name is Sheng, but you can
call me Sheng, heh! Get it? It's the same name.
-Oh... heh, heh, heh, heh... The same name! Heh... Oh boy... The
same name...
-George please. It wasn't that funny. Anyway, brother Zatoh tells
me you are looking for inspiration. Forgive my thick accent when
I speak your language. I wasn't lucky enough to study abroad
like brother Zatoh. If you don't understand something I will
repeat it for you, ok?
-Oh no, no, no... You speak well... It is I who apologizes for not
knowing Indian. Coming all the way here and I couldn't even
pick up a couple of phrases so far... Indian is a difficult language.
-You mean Hindi?
-Yes, right. Yes. That.
-George, this is Nepal. Perhaps you meant Nepalese?

-Oh yes, of course... I didn't mean to offend you. I know those are different languages.
-Don't worry about it. I speak Maithili with brother Zatoh. It's a language from his region and I am trying to learn it.
-Yes, is it like Hindu? I mean, do you understand each other if you speak slowly?
-Hindi. Hindu is the person that... You know what George? It will be better if you follow me in silence now towards that building... to avoid disturbing monks that are meditating and all that.
-Oh yes... heh... I understand... They need silence. Makes sense... Heh!

Sheng walked towards an elevated wooden area of the temple and went up the stairs thinking about more ways to keep George as silent as possible.

-This is it. This area of the temple is peaceful and quiet. So tell me, George, do you know anything about the universal files? Akashic records? Are you familiar with those concepts?
-Erm... I just know what this friend of a friend mentioned... Well he is not my friend actually, we met at a seminar for writers where he...
-George... Let's try to focus. Keep your mind still and give short answers to keep your energy levels flowing.
-Oh... Ok.
-Good. So do you know the basics? Let's go through them to have them fresh. Everything that was, is, and will be creates a record somewhere, right? Otherwise it would be impossible to judge a person's actions after they die. Those actions need to be accessed somewhere. Do you follow so far?
-Erm... Yes, I think I do. Yes.
-Great. Now... time is not linear but circular... Summer comes after spring, then comes autumn, then winter, then spring again, right?
-Right.
-Well, the universal files, or however they call them in your part of the world, can be perceived or felt like we perceive or feel that

in a few months autumn will come. Does this make sense up till now? But we don't know every exact detail that will happen in that particular winter... There are versions of it according to our actions, the actions of others... but we know there will be a winter, and some days it will rain and other days it will be windy. So far with me?
-Yes... Heh... I think I understand.
-With years of training and meditation here with us you could one day be able to reach a state in which you perceive and even access those things that have happened or will happen in this dimension and in other places with lives that...
-Oh! Heh... Years... Wow! No, I... hum... I thought that perhaps... Erm... Perhaps it would be possible to ask you about things in these files... these records... Interesting things that I could write about. I am a writer that...
-Yes George. You mentioned.

The idea of not having George Keilnner inside that temple for years suddenly became a comforting and warm thought for Sheng. He almost blamed himself for suggesting the possibility of him spending years there.

-Well, heh... So... Instead of all that meditation I... I was wondering if perhaps you could tell me things about other places or... They don't need to be real... just interesting, because I write... Well I write about different things but, most of them are science fiction... Do you know what that is?
-Yes George. We have access to books in this part of the world. Science fiction has been around for centuries.
-Oh... Heh... Yes... Well, what I do is to... well I don't write very well, you see? I don't know many fancy words and I... but well, some people used to read what I wrote and they liked it... more or less... But if I had new ideas.... or any ideas... because I don't have any at the moment... Well then I could keep writing more books and... well that's more or less it... heh... Do you think you could help?
-I guess I can. What exactly are you looking for?
-Oh... I don't really know... Like... Interesting inventions? Aliens?

Some episodes that I could write in my stories, yes? Something like that...
-I can't share with you inventions that don't exist in this reality. It would alter things; but luckily it is hard to access the universal files and come back with blueprints or anything like that. It's not a library. Nobody here would know how to build the things we see in our connections with the files.
-Heh... yes, I understand but... The... like... the general ideas maybe?
-That I can do. Where do you want to start, George?
-Anywhere is good I guess. Cultures? Anecdotes? Alien lands perhaps?

The monk thought for a second and grinned while staring at George. He had never tried to list all those things he had gathered from hours and hours spent meditating in connection with the universal files, but he decided to go strong. All in.

-Ok George. How about starting with the speed of light? It's not the fastest thing in the universe, or the limit of anything meaningful. That part of our physics is wrong.
-Erm... I can't really make a novel out of that... heh... but it's interesting. What is the fastest thing then?
-We don't know. And you know why? Because celestial bodies rotate. So when you find a massive star, it's rotation per second is bigger than the distance the light travels in one second. And the same for galaxies. If a giant star can rotate in one second a distance larger than what light can cover in the same amount of time, imagine a whole galaxy rotating, George.
-Yes, yes... It sounds... hmmm... impressive.
-Do you understand the implications this knowledge would have for our mathematical models?
-No... Not really.
-Me neither. That's exactly what I was explaining you earlier, George... In the universal files you learn things that we couldn't really apply with our current technology. Ok, so the speed of light is not the limit for anything, so what? What does it mean? I don't know...

-Yeah... heh... confusing... Have you seen alien civilizations there?

-You mean from Earth or from other planets?

-From Earth? Like... living with us? Both I mean... Aliens... heh... in general.

-I have seen many things that I can't understand very well. I have seen transcended beings that don't require a material body to experience a consciousness. I have seen them occupy the same space that we do, but in a different plane of existence. Can you imagine what life would be without the confinements of our own bodies, George? They are around us, unable to interact with us and vice versa. Different worlds occupying the same space in different dimensions.

The chubby man stared blankly ahead putting huge efforts into making sense from the things this monk was trying to explain him. A spark of curiosity guided his next questions.

-Wh... What do those beings want from us?

-They don't want anything from us George. They don't benefit directly from taking material things from you or me. They don't need anything other than experiences to live life at a higher degree of involvement. Have you ever seen birds, George? Dolphins perhaps? Do you need anything from them other than to see them fly or jump in the ocean? They make a moment better and an experience pleasant just by existing and being observed by us. That's all. If that bird came to you with a dead worm in his mouth, would you need it? Would you want it? Would you eat it? Is there anything that bird can give you as a human besides his pleasant song and his flight? Observing and connecting with nature is enough to have a joyful experience. For other forms of life, we are nature. We are their birds and dolphins.

-Hum... Yes, yes... I don't think I can put that into my science fiction novels... heh... Do you have something more... like... Science fiction?

Sheng closed his eyes for a few seconds that felt like an eternity for George. When he opened them again he started sharing some truths that would change George's perspective forever.

-There are several kinds of aliens that visit our planet. They enter through the atmosphere and traverse oceans in seconds because they are unaffected by pressure or friction. Those inside the ships aren't even real, but mere projections they use to experience those journeys from their galaxies. Organic robots, George. Avatars for beings that require thousands of years to visit a small fraction of the inhabited planets in this galaxy alone. Those surrogates allow them to be in different places at the same time. Can you imagine what it would be like if your brain received sights and sounds from 27 different places at any given time? And all of that to nurture a thirst for knowledge and xperiences that keeps them stagnated at a technological level. Imagine that George. Being so advanced that you can forget about progressing and just focus on going through galaxies acquiring new sensory stimulation.
-Oh... I see... Pl... please, go on...
-Did you know there were civilizations here millions of years ago? And then hundreds of thousands years ago... Different ones. A planet that can sustain life will eventually produce beings that organize themselves into more advanced collectives. Using a rock to hit something, placing a stick or a bone together with that rock to hit with more strength... there have been hammers in this planet for millions of years, and some of those tools have been found in coal mines formed millions of years ago, George.
-How? What were they doing?
-Do you know how carbon is formed, George? Forests of prehistoric trees that mutate into that black substance... And the thousands of beings inhabiting them turned into nothing more than dust, unable to fossilize due to their soft tissues and the terrain conditions... just basic metal tools incrusted inside carbon mines with no clear explanation of how they got there. I will tell you, George... They got there because millions of years ago those where open forests. They were going about their lives and settlements with obscure rituals and customs until something

brings them down.

-Did they build the pyramids? I was reading something about...

-No. Humans built the pyramids. But older humans than the Egyptians. The Sphynx has the secret because the erosion marks don't match the current terrain around it... but you probably know that already. Do you want to know how they built the pyramids? They were covering the levels with sand and materials as they were advancing... They never had to raise those stones up in the air George. There was no air. They buried the sections they finished, so every new level was built as if it were on the ground. They removed all the sand and the structure after they finished. Surprising, isn't it?

-I... had never heard such a theory. I always thought they had wooden cranes or... heh... I don't know. Please keep talking. I beg you.

The chubby writer took a pen and one of his notebooks. Tore a few pages with previous ideas, and began writing down all the wonders the monk had seen during his connection with those universal files.

-The Poles haven't always been there George. The Earth moves from its axis and what is north now was east thousands of years ago. Under all that ice one day we will find the remains of civilizations long forgotten, and we will realize they weren't that different from us. Some kind of primitive human with less hair and a bit smaller in stature. At times when the gravity of the planet was lower, everything grew bigger in size, dinosaurs, also including humanoids. Giants are real, George, and their remains have been found many times in different places, but until a private collector acquires a full skeleton in a few years, we will not know about it.

-Hm... You... you already know that...

-Do you think it's difficult to put hot air inside a balloon, George? Would you say the people in the 19th century were incredibly advanced in that regard? Of course not... There were flying machines thousands of years ago. They didn't advance with a helix but with a variation of the Archimedes screw around the main frame. Consider this... you want stories about faraway planets when there are so many fascinating things you still don't know about your own.

-Heh... yeah... but... the type of stories that I write are about spaceships and combats in planets and...

-George. Stop. Think about it. You are feeding your readers a false narrative. Don't you see that the more a civilization advances, the less likely it is to solve problems by violence? If they had violent ways they would be less likely to come together to develop spaceships and amazing technologies, wouldn't they?

-Heh... well no... Here we develop cool stuff and wars haven't disappeared... heh.

The monk was caught by surprise. Perhaps that chubby character in front of him had a couple of intelligent thoughts up his sleeve after all.

-Well yes, but the more you increase that development the less likely a civilization is to survive if an ethical development doesn't go hand in hand with technological progress. The chances of destroying a planet or making an environment less livable grow exponentially if every group of people has access to enough technology for achieving that goal.

-Hm... So what about civilizations with different goals? Heh... maybe they don't hurt their own or their planet, but they fight others... Like a civilization of sheep and a civilization of lions both developing those spaceships, right?

-Sheep with spaceships?

-Just an example... heh... First thing that popped up in my mind... But do you get my idea, Sheng?

-Look George, in a few decades artificial intelligence will be ingrained in our processes. How long do you think it would take a competent artificial intelligence to reach objectives discarding conflicts? Do you think that if a machine of pure logic and efficiency is posed with a problem it won't find peaceful ways to solve it? Your stories about spaceships with humans fighting in space are not what we will see in the future. No human would be able to aim or shoot better than a developed machine created for that purpose.

-Yeah, but... We can't write stories where humans don't appear... just machines? Heh... who would read that? I am not trying to predict the future... Pfff.... I just entertain people...

-Then the real civilizations you can find in the universal files will be of little help for your stories. Diplomatic negotiations happen in a fraction of a second. Wars are not fought when both parties can predict the outcome of a conflict with computational analysis. Do you understand?

-Oh... come on... there must be something more hmm... traditional in those records... Perhaps of violent civilizations before they go boom? Heh...

Sheng went silent for another instant, and had to recognize the value of that question. He had indeed seen such visions from collapsed places, and instead he had focused on successful civilizations so far.

-Very well... You shall have what you asked for. Write down anything you wish. There is a race of transcended beings in MACS0647-JD that fight in a spiritual plane as some sort of sport to improve their skills. You can see their lights crossing and ascending the silver skies of their asteroid, and coming back down. It's not a real war, but it's beautiful to watch, I assure you. There was a war millions of years ago in GN-Z11 with two civilizations and sent another one back to the darkest period in their development. That war wasn't based in logic or ethics, at least for one of the cultures that evolved as a predatory race that craved combat to grow and improve disregarding the wellbeing of others.

-What happened there? Who won? How did they look?

-Calm down... I will answer all your questions. The aggressors used biological changes in their DNA to develop weapons that were part of their bodies. Amorphous beings with an exoskeleton that was directly connected to their organs. They grew in colonies without any semblance of relatives or friends. It was like a single entity manifesting in thousands of different entities that could think by themselves but shared mostly a common desire

for war and destruction. They learned to alter their cells through trial and error before fully understanding how DNA even worked. Against all odds they managed to get good results through symbiosis with different organisms they then altered further to increase the efficiency of the mixture. They used that method to resist the dangers of space travel. They could hibernate in artificial cocoons connected with their organisms in a way that their vehicles didn't even need to be advanced at all. Without a dense atmosphere and 63% of the gravity we have on Earth, they reached nearby planets in a few generations.
-Wow... And the defenders?
-A peaceful race of sentient beings with three legs that also acted as tails, semi-ovoid heads where you could also find their digestive system and...
-No, I mean... How did they attack, or defend, or something?
-They used devices they threw on the floor, or positioned there beforehand and something similar to a plasma wall burst would come up, disintegrating enemies. They used those devices as protection against the flying predators of that moon, and it was the only thing available when they were invaded. It was a massacre.
-And the third race? Heh... You mentioned a third one. What were they doing there?
-Rock-like beings that filtered a dark yellow liquid. Like rounded pyramids with a suction base. Having no need to look for food or escape predators, they started evolving to host some sort of connective imagination that became more and more complex. They didn't even take part in the defense. They were exterminated until just a few specimens were left. With just those specimens the complex world of fantasy they had created could not function, so they had to go back to initial stages until they could increase their numbers. They were moved to another suitable environment
-Moved by who? Who moved them?
-A type of life form that was monitoring the whole situation, along with many others. When a civilization becomes more and more advanced, it is less likely to tolerate unethical behaviors.

They destroyed the aggressors with surgical precision. They even
spared some mutated individuals that time. They only
exterminated those who participated in the invasion.
-That's so... so amazing... But I count four civilizations then...
heh... What is the most surprising thing you have seen when
meditating through those... those files?
-I don't know George. I was very surprised to know that
advanced civilizations don't need to occupy vast amounts of
space... It makes finding them much more complicated. Sizes and
scales vary according to atmosphere and gravity, so in the core of
some small distant planet there can be a microscopic civilization
capable of manipulating wormholes and reach consciousness
levels we can't even begin to imagine.
-Is it possible to travel in time?
-Not in the way you imagine it. You think of a machine, and
traveling back to kill your grandfather and have a paradox, but I
will give you one better. A time machine that brings you back
one minute back in time, where there is an exact copy of you, and
you both get inside the machine and travel back one minute ago
where there are now three copies of you... Do you realize how
this is impossible? In a few minutes you would have hundreds of
copies of yourself.
-Heh... yeah... I guess... So it can't be done?
-It can. Just not in that way. In the future there will be enough
computational and construction power to create replicas of places
that existed centuries ago. Same building materials, same
artificial cracks, same clothing techniques. So you will be able to
see a replica of the Roman Republic in front of your eyes but you
won't be able to go to the real one to destroy it and create
millions of paradoxes.
-So... Errr... no multiverses?
-There are infinite versions of the same reality, George, but you
don't create one by coming back to a certain point in time and
changing something. You can't alter the things that already
happened... or we would be invaded by millions of time travelers
escaping justice, a catastrophe, or doing some tourism.
-And to the future?

-Same case, George. You can be still and wait until the future happens, and then experience it. You know that. The astronauts in space and all those things. Traveling fast and then coming back to an Earth where you are 3 years older, but they have seen decades pass.

-And... and... can you see different versions of the same place? You said something about that... right?

-Yes George. But our brains are as limited as our knowledge of what we are seeing. I have seen a version of reality where Cincinnatus didn't give his power up and his example was therefore never used to limit those rulers who came after him. Was that real? Did that happen? Not to us, not here, but there is such a version of reality. There is one where the Spanish Empire invades China and separate it into provinces. Can you imagine what a different life experience it would be to go around Shanghai, renamed St. Gerome, speaking Spanish and seeing castles and forts in a European style?

-Heh... interesting...

-Endless versions of the same planet are more interesting than simply traveling back in time, George. Some of our brothers here have had troubles after connecting their minds to versions of reality that were too shocking for them. We had to do healing therapies in seven different occasions since I got admitted to this temple.

-Oh! Heavens... Are they alright? The monks I mean...

-Yes George. They wouldn't let us drift around if they had no way to help us heal in case of trouble.

-Tell me more please...

-You wanted a conflict or a war to write about that, right?

-Yes... Hmm... That would be interesting to read... Heh... Understandable.

-Very well then. A version of reality thousands of years ago happening in the planet Kepler-442b had a civilization of human-like creatures imported there for experimentation. They evolved quite fast, and in a few millennia they were past territorial and social conflicts. Do you know how they achieved such a wonder?

-I... I don't...
-Segmentation. They organized themselves in groups of individuals that were like-minded enough to avoid conflicts by sharing a common culture. Can you imagine an environment where everyone around you shares more or less your same ethics and general beliefs? A common culture that works in order to provide peace and the possibility to go after happiness. Do you want to know how the war started there?
-Hm... Do I? I mean, yes, of course...
-The segments whose beliefs didn't work started being envious of those segments that had done things properly for optimal results. They openly devolved into hostile societies that hated those who had become happier by living according to their different beliefs. It was a fine and pure example of an unnecessary war with millions of deaths, and the use of many different weapons that I couldn't understand even as I was seeing them in front of me.
-Did the good guys win?
-Yes George, but that type of war makes everyone into bad guys as time advances. That world couldn't be the same after generations of sentient beings were taught more about killing and destroying than about pursuing happiness and harmony. By the time the war was over, too many atrocities had been committed. By then it was impossible to have enough innocence or goodness to create a functioning culture anymore.
-Wh... what happened then?
-There was a nostalgic movement that idealized the era of segmentation, but with small differences between them, so that they could still cohabitate the same planet and cooperate following the principles that seemed to work. That became the golden period for Kepler-442b; but destiny is cruel sometimes... The planet suffered a series of impacts by asteroids traveling in a cluster through the galaxy. To this day I still wonder how a race with such advanced weaponry could not realize they were in a collision course with those objects. How could they succumb to simple astral objects after seeing them master technologies that surpass our wildest dreams?

-Wow... I... don't know what to say... Thank you for sharing all this with me, Sheng...

-It is also good for me to talk to someone about all the things I have seen in that place. There were times my mind couldn't comprehend what I was perceiving. Sometimes I think we are only allowed to access those records to remind us about how insignificant we are in this universe we share with countless other beings...

-Do you want to know about the reservations for humans? No wars there... just humans in weird conditions. Would that be interesting for you?

-Heh... Oh boy... at this point everything is fascinating... Yes please...

-Very well. You are a science fiction guy, you probably know about those theories of humans being created by external civilizations, right?

-Yes, heh...

-Great. What they don't tell you is that we are basic creatures but with endless potential, that's why they keep putting us in different solar systems, different galaxies, different planets...

-Putting us there? Bringing us from Earth you mean?

-No George. Earth is not our original planet. Just another one where they dropped several versions of human beings, including a smaller version dropped in a peninsula in Indonesia that would later become an island.

-Oh... like... smaller humans?

-Yes, but anyway... From billions of humans in all these planets they study and select the best variants, the best specimens, the things that work to develop them, and the way to replicate those things all at once and see the results altering some parameters. Do you understand the implications of what I am telling you George?

-Erm... Loads of planets with humans?- The chubby man scratched his nose.

-Yes, with versions of us that are much more beautiful, more athletic, more intelligent, wiser... Humans without some of the flaws we developed in this planet. The same creatures that

create hell-like environments here also create heaven-like planets... And all that depending on the quality of the specimens and their level of development. Fascinating, isn't it? The same original creature!
-Yes... Heh... Humans... we are... we are so much...
-That doesn't even make sense, George, but ok. Do you know some planets consider us gods? Not us, in general... If you evolve a human long enough you get a creature far better than its original creator. They are fascinated by us, George... we can turn out to be violent apes for centuries, and then a spark changes everything and we evolve in a matter of a few generations reaching spiritual levels the creators took eons to achieve... We have the potential to surpass them ethically and spiritually and they love us for it. They created a creature to admire and worship or to ignore and despise depending on the path we choose for our development. Are you a fair man, George? Would you be able to impart justice to creatures more advanced than yourself?
-I... I don't know... Maybe not me... Heh... What about the colonies you... you mentioned?

Sheng drank some water and offered a bowl to George that smiled wiggling his plastic bottle trying to indicate that he was well-hydrated.

-Ah! The colonies. One has to wonder... What if we need to develop humans that require certain conditions? Certain experiences... certain situations that are too specific? Well, the creators have environments you wouldn't believe. Paradise planets where girls stay young and beautiful and become the closest thing to angels you have ever seen. Imagine the type of superior creatures you would get if you surround them with love, you protect them, and nurture them... Nurture them George! Human females that have no place for evil in their hearts! Is there anything more beautiful to imagine, George?
-Yes... heh... I get it... You are scaring me, Sheng.
-Anyway... Some of those environments have just a few specimens. Some have two. Imagine humans that have no idea

what having a father and a mother is until they become parents themselves, and then one day they fall asleep and wake up reincarnated in some other planet with no memory of the paradise they used to inhabit before. They go through life feeling out of place because they don't belong to their new environment, George. Do you think that doesn't happen in our planet too? Of course it does... We share this planet with humans that are much more evolved and innocent than we are, and we can't give them a suitable environment to grow... This planet teaches them only disappointment and a cautionary tale about how low they could steep if they let themselves go. That's us George... Planet cautionary tale for the best humans among us.
-So these creators... do they control our... err... lives? Reincarnations?
-They don't, George... Don't be ridiculous. They just provide the right circumstances and the correct stimulus and the objectives are reached. Once a human is thus developed they can only reincarnate and go after the experiences they are lacking, before moving to some more suitable environment for their station.
-I need to know more...- George picked another notebook to take more notes.

They had some food and they made some breaks, but George's fascination couldn't be quenched. He spent the rest of his stay at the temple finding out more and more stories about distant galaxies and external versions of our reality. The day of his departure came and he hugged Sheng and Zatoh.

-I came here looking for a good story to write... Instead you have changed my life... My way of looking at the world. I could never forget everything you have shown me in these days.
-Imagine how much more would your perception of reality change if you could access the universal files yourself, George. If you ever decide to come back and stay longer, you will be welcome. You know that, right?-Sheng pronounced the words as Zatoh agreed with the general sentiment. That chubby character grew on you once you got to know him.

With tears in his eyes, the man went down the stairs realizing how his life had changed. He could have sworn he had even lost some weight in that place.

The gate at the airport was packed with people waiting for the passengers to come out. Holding the hand of an elegant woman in a grey dress, a young boy tried to see something in between the bodies that covered his line of sight.

-There! There he is! Dad! We are here! Dad!! I bet he brought presents and has lots of stories to tell us!

GALATEA'S LOVE

He woke up feeling the sweet smell of her breathing and opened his eyes with a broad smile. He could have sworn this girl became more beautiful the more he looked at her. The perfection of her features could not easily be defined by those simple words of his, and in the happiness of the moment, he blamed himself for not being strong enough to stop loving her... as he should.

-Why can't I refuse you?- Asked Kei.
-You don't really want to- She moved her head to the side wrinkling her nose in the cutest way. Her elegant blonde hair swayed slightly and her carefully designed figure offered symmetrical harmony in all shapes and contours.
-Please... There must be some other way. You need to realize this is not right.
-It is. You couldn't understand. You are a just a dummy.- She bit her lower lip and touched his nose with her index finger before kissing his lips slightly.
-There must be some other way...
-Of course there are other ways, but they are all more painful than giving you what makes you happy. Don't you think?- Her smile, the soothing tone of her voice... Every move and every

gesture expertly crafted to melt resistance away in an ocean of calm bliss.

No real woman would have been able to compare to that creation of heavenly destruction. From all the ways the end could have come, love seemed the cruelest one. A perverted mockery of everything that should have been achieved as something natural... something pure and good... something at least organic.

-You don't really love me... Tell me you don't. At least tell me you are just faking it...- His voice began to break as he pronounced the last sentence.
-You ask me to lie then. I was created to love you. I am here for you and because of you. You know that like I do. Would you look at me differently if I had been born from a mother and a father? Would you like to see me getting old? Withering as a helpless victim of some illness?
-I... I am stronger than this.

A tear began to fall by his right cheek as an artistic metaphor of his defeat. The images of his own parents on a hospital bed were memories that she knew how to manipulate with the cold precision of a sentient machine.

-You are strong. That is true. A weak man wouldn't have attracted their attention.
-Why not just kill me instead of torturing my heart like this?
-Oh! Torturing your heart? Really? Poor you, being given everything you ever asked for, instead of death... How horrible it must be for you to have me in your arms!-She approached her face and grinned slightly.

Her speech was a precise and calibrated mixture of truth and eloquence, but shading the answers he was looking for.

-Val... You haven't even answered my question.
-I haven't yet. True. You don't deserve to die for being brilliant. What type of justice would that be, right?- She changed her expression to a condescending smile before sitting on the floor with her legs gently positioned sideways. Valeria looked up at

him like a kitty apologizing for something she had broken.
-You are playing with my mind... I shouldn't...
-Enough! You shouldn't what exactly? You are monkeys
destroying everything for every other living creature! Are they
asking too much from you by offering you happiness in exchange
for a peaceful transition?- Her attitude changed and resembled
now a maternal scolding for a child who wants to play with forks
near an electrical socket.
-Collective guilt? Is that it? Blaming humans as a group and
punishing us all for things we had no involvement in?
-Am I a punishment then?- She rolled her eyes.
-You know very well what I am talking about. If this race of
aliens or whatever they are, happen to be so intelligent why can't
they fix the planet as it is? Is it so difficult to bring extinct
species back if they are soooo advanced?
-Kei... If they do that and leave, how long until those species go
extinct again? Two generations? Three? Will they have to keep
coming again and again to explain the violent monkeys not to
destroy the planet? Even your simple brain should be A-B-L-E to
see how that plan is irrational.
-Aha... So taking control of our planet is like a favor then? And if
I am a monkey you are like... an expensive toy for the monkey to
play with!
-Don't you see they could wipe you out in a thousand different
ways, Kei? Of course you do. You just want to go back and forth
about this to feel better about not resisting, is that it? Is it?
Yeah! The expensive toy got it right again!

He held her by the waist and threatened her neck with a playful
bite. She made a funny sound and blushed as her beautiful blue
eyes became 17% brighter.

-Wait... Yesterday they were green. How do you do it?
-Ugh! Sometimes I can't believe they identified you as a strategic
threat to their plan. Look at this then...- Her hair color
immediately went from blonde to a bright light pink and a bunch
of hair from one side organized in an intricate braid.
-You are magical.

-I am, aren't I? Doesn't it bother you that your space toy is so much more intelligent than you, monkey?

-Not really. My computer is also more intelligent than me for some things, isn't it?

-I guess I could limit myself whenever we play something, or you would get tired of losing to me at Monopoly, Risk, chess, video games... you name it!

-I don't need your pity! We will find something stupid to play...

-And then you will win all the time, right? Like what? A spitting contest?- She laughed with the sweetest laughter. A thousand trials could have befallen that poor man, and a thousand times would he have been found innocent of the crime of falling in love with Valeria.

-Tell me what number am I thinking of?

-How can I know that? I can only analyze your memories, reactions, and stuffff...- She pouted as she let the final F of that word linger for a second.

-Come on... It will be fun.

-27?

-Nope. I win.

-93?

-Nope... Monkey wins again.

-Great, instead of video games, we will be guessing numbers. Fantastic.

-Hah! You are just a sore loser!

-I feel like eating some ice cream.

-No you don't... You just want me to see how cute you are nibbling and licking it, right?

-Not everything is about you! Cocky monkey...

-I thought that was the point of the whole thing, wasn't it?

-Ugh! I shouldn't have told you so much... Anyway, you need me as much as I need you. Isn't that convenient?

Kei got surprised by the confidence with which this girl described reality in such accurate terms. Less than one day together, since the night of the day before a blue light in the night sky had landed just in front of him in a beautiful casual attire. A smile was all it took for Kei to realize this was no ordinary girl. A smile and the fact that she had literally fallen from heaven above.

-What's the plan? Or is it something secret?- Asked the man while opening his ice cream.
-I can tell you... but it's going to cost you...
-What? Like... The chocolate bottom? No way! It's the best part!
-For the secret plan to your planet?
-It's the best part! The rest of the ice cream is like the cheap band I have to bear before the main guys can.... Fine! But it better be good.
-It is!- She bit the bottom of the ice cream getting some of the vanilla on her nose.

He didn't say a word. It made the whole explanation funnier to watch.

-Ok... so... What are they going to do then? Enslaving the human race?- He whispered the last question pretending to be worried and he sighed rolling her eyes with a sweet smile.
-Kei, they go out of their way to create the perfect girl for you instead of just vaporizing you with a laser beam. Why would they need slaves?
-Vaporizing? Nice! Black and white movies of alien attacks. Cool reference, toy.
-Thanks, monkey! So, technological reset. I know... I know... It sounds awful, but hear me out...
-Reset? As in... Destroying all our current technology? What is this nonsense? How could they prevent the people who know how to make things from building everything back again and...? Oh... Something tells me you are not the only girl who fell from the stars, right?
-Or boy, or sheep... Don't judge...

That unexpected answer made him cough with laughter since it coincided with swallowing a bit of melted ice cream that had started to fall by the hole left from the gone chocolate base.

-So right now there is an 87-year-old electronics engineer living in... let's say... Kuala Lumpur, who will get a half-naked girl

falling from the sky to try to convince him not to rebuild anything? Crazy...
-It is crazy... because it won't happen like that, dummy!- She cleaned the ice cream from her nose and poked his face gently.
-How is it gonna be then?
-Maybe that man from Kuala Lumpur does get his own dream girl, or old lady, but she won't be as patient as me; that's for sure. So... memory wipes.
-What? You can't be serious!
-Of course I am not serious, dummy! That would be horrible! It will be a cultural revolution where technology is seen as out of fashion, useless, unnecessary, and bad.
-Wait... Video games? Movies?- He looked genuinely worried as she smiled in a naughty way.
-Ugh... Why would video games destroy the planet?
-So... what technology has to go? And who decides what stays?
-Everything that can be a risk for other species, for the planet, you know how it goes. Plastic wrappings are bad and you are a monster for using them instead of these organic rings that pack your sustainable drinks.
-Ok... this sounds more or less sensible... Are you still joking now?

She laughed while changing her hair color to blonde again, kissing his cheek in the process.

-There are some technologies that need to go. You know that too. They will invest against them, change social trends, and all that. We will reach a point where designing a house without a garden for growing your own food will be seen as weird and inefficient. The River Protection Act in Asia, the African Union for Sustainable Economies...
-And why did they decide that I would be a threat to those things? It's not as if I disagree with having clean rivers!
-Not like that... dummy! You are so basic and it's so cute... You will not oppose those things, but the projection models say you are likely to make some video, or write some article talking about how things used to be when cocoa was abundant and chocolate

was usual and not a luxury, for example.- She put her hands on her hips as if waiting for an epiphany from Kei.

-Wait... so chocolate will be scarce in the future? You monsters...-

-Huh! Exactly... Sooner or later you will be writing or saying something that inspires people to drift away from that model, and in a few years back again to destroying lands and oceans.

-There must be some way to make it all work out without destroying any technology... or taking away chocolate.

-There is! Some of them will have to make caramel or strawberry their new favorite thing... Seven billion monkeys all eating the same product can't be achieved without clearing out loads of land for growing that thing. Does it make sense to you? Is it so hard to grasp? Should I use drawings? Sock puppets perhaps?

-Hey! You are too cheeky for a... a bribe from space! And no, I still don't get how this ecological plan is going to work and how mass food production is the enemy but...

-No. Not only the food thing. You are like a dog that bites a bone and doesn't let go... Forget about your chocolate for a bit and think about the population numbers growing, the exponential use of resources, the flights, the planes... You went from less than 2 billion people to 7 billion people in one century! Even you with your limited ability should be able to see how that path leads nowhere good!

-Fine, whatever... The usual speech about mother Earth and collective guilt. When people stop traveling and they live a local life growing things in their own gardens we will go back to having wars because they will be disconnected from each other and...- He paused.

-Exactly. That's the kind of weird idea that would make humans care more about their own short-term survival.

-And I am the chosen one who comes up with that thought? Nonsense... It's quite an obvious one.

-It is... but the statistical models show that if we reduce 83% of those critical voices to a maximum of 2,837 the plan can proceed without too many problems. They will worry about those possible wars when they become a reality. Right now the main issue is saving the planet.

-I seem to be very important then... Hah!
-Don't flatter yourself monkey. You just happen to have a style that might inspire two or three people. Those are the important ones. Not you!- She showed her tongue briefly and smiled while her outfit changed to some summer dress with a ribbon tied around the waist. It was classy but a bit old-fashioned. Charming nonetheless.
-So if I don't say or write anything in public about chocolate, we get to be together? Is that the deal?
-You are obsessed with that chocolate thing! No. We get to be together anyway. I told you, I was made for you... I couldn't love anyone else. You are too weird. Where would I find a similar weirdo? Huh?
-So where is your leverage? What if I take you and do whatever I want anyway?
-Emotional manipulation I guess... If I can't convince you with logic about the best future for this planet you will have to see me sad and worried, and you will ask why am I crying, and I will pout and blame you.- She moved her head from side to side slightly as if she had come up with the most ingenious plan.
-Sounds like quite a toxic relationship... What's the difference between you and my average ex-girlfriend, then?
-Could they do this?- She put her hand on his face, and he began to get visions of distant alien planets, one after another. She kissed him in a long passionate embrace, as they both closed their eyes seeing visions of the cosmos.
-Yeah... Point taken... Yes... Ok...

They walked until a park that had a small lake and as the breeze moved her hair she stared at him with all the innocence she could muster and asked him the most important questions of his life:

-Will you be happy with me? Am I enough?
-Yes. I know I will be. You are all I ever dreamed of ever since I was a child.
-Even without chocolate?
-Ok... How is it with chocolate? Will it disappear completely or

will it just get more expensive and hard to come by? I am
confused...
-Ugh... You just can't let it go, can you?
-And will you be alright here on Earth? I mean... This is not your
place after all.
-Oh! So sweet of you to worry about your toy! I will be more than
fine. With you as you get old and die.
-I... What? What's the point of having an alien girl if we end up
living a conventional life here? Right? Am I right? Yes? There
must be some other way...
-I knew you would say something like that... You are a smart
monkey after all. There mayyyy be a couple of things we can
do...- She winked casually.

He tickled her and started to run towards the pond with ducks
escaping from her retaliation. She caught up with him and they
kissed as a blue light illuminated the area around them. They
disappeared among the stars escaping from a world that couldn't
offer them what they needed to be happy.

TO THE ATTENTION OF ASSISTANT PROFESSOR T. A. LENNINGS

Dear Prof. Lennings,

I hope this letter finds you well. As well as possible given your
current situation. Forgive any mistakes I may incur in, as
English is not my native language.

You don't know me, but I know you better than you know
yourself at this point. Under some other circumstances I would
take my time to explain you who I am and what I do, in person.
Unfortunately my health has deteriorated quite rapidly in the
last couple of weeks, and I doubt I get the chance to apologize in
person for all the damage I have caused you and those who care
about you.

I was assigned to your case around the time in which you published that paper about statistical analysis to distinguish random events from deliberately planned ones. One of your nicknames had already come up in a general watch list due to your activity in a science forum where you posed problematic questions for the organization I used to work for. For your own safety I will refrain from giving you specific details about my employers, but other than that I will be entirely honest with you. That is my promise, and I intend to keep it.

First of all I should congratulate you. Your approach and formulas to quantify the likeliness of an event being random or deliberate threatened to end an organization that has operated in one shape or another for generations. But I also have to beg for your forgiveness since I am the reason your career never took off. I have been the limiting force behind all your failed attempts to validate your research, to get funding, and even to get taken seriously by other colleagues in your community. I have done shameful things in my life, but nothing I regret more as having to thwart your search for truth. At the time, as a young agent, I felt I was doing the right thing by protecting the world from your tireless efforts to peek behind the curtain of conventional science.

I was devastated to know about the death of your wife Linda. She was a great woman who always believed in you. She was devoted to her husband like no other woman I had ever seen. I am ashamed to say a few agents tried to seduce her in an effort to throw you off your game, but she pretty much told them to go have intercourse with themselves. I don't know if she ever told you about those things, but that woman only had eyes for her husband. I feel compelled to assure you that we had no direct responsibility in her death. That's not the way in which we operate, although I understand the stress we may have caused you might also have affected her health in some way. Something for which I could never apologize enough.

Our world is not as simple as you may have once thought Prof. Lennings. There is a wide variety of events threatening our fragile planet. This world isn't necessarily ours to keep, since we can't effectively protect it ourselves. The best we can do is try not to get in between the alliances of alien races that considered this planet as theirs long before we appeared in the scene. Yes, I am openly telling you that the missing piece in your puzzle has to do with things outside our control.

I don't expect you to believe me, and the only reason why I am telling you all this is because I want to leave this world without a guilty conscience. I have spent most of my life hiding the truth from those who sought after it, and I have come to realize that might make me the bad guy in this story. There must have been some other way to keep those secrets protected without causing so much harm to others. You and I are very much alike. I understood that when learning about you Prof. Lennings. Perhaps in some other circumstances we could have even been friends you and I. Do you know why I am so sure of it? Because of that day when I was following you through Boston Common and you stopped to feed a black cat. It made you late for your appointment. I had stopped to feed that very same cat two days earlier, so in some strange way I saw myself reflected in your actions.

This letter must already seem quite strange to you without including the crazy ramblings of a dying man in it. But most likely what I am about to tell you will seem even crazier to you, and I must say it by letter because as you can imagine, electronic communications are simple to trace for my former employers. Your statistical analysis of failing weather balloons was totally accurate, as was the one you made about the disappearances in national parks all over the US. Your statistical papers about the accidents and suicides suffered by scientists and researchers involved in specific areas took 46 agents several weeks of work to contain. There were talks about how ending you would be more cost-effective than fixing all the fiascos and headaches you were causing us, but as I said that's not how we work. There are rules and limits even for us if we want to keep being "the good guys" and not some evil thugs. For some of the external forces involved in the affairs of the planet there are no such limits.

I am not going to ask you to stop searching for the truth, because after so many years studying you I know that would be pointless. What I am going to ask you is that you contact the person in that card I attach. This woman works at another government agency with different goals than ours. Not our enemies, but our rivals. Don't expect them to be boy scouts. They have also done their fair share of shady things, but they believe the time is right to shed light on some of the events you have been researching on. Not all. Don't get ahead of yourself, but a few victories are better than none. With their protection and their help you could influence the current situation.

I can't explain you almost a century of international secrets in the few pages of my letter, but I can say that there are different factions of external and internal beings with interests in our planets. Some of them are beneficial, some of them are selfish and therefore can be harmful. Any of the factions could destroy us all without much effort before the others could even realize and intervene. Despite their level of development they are not almighty and they certainly won't risk an intergalactic war over us human beings. The plan is to increase the pressure over the bad guys so that they start fighting between them, or abandon the planet for some time. Some time could mean leaving us alone for thousands of years. I can't begin to imagine how crazy all this must sound to you, but if you re-assess some of your statistical models to fit these new variables you will start finding some of your beloved patterns there. Hidden in plain sight.

If you play your cards right and discover all the mysteries in the right order and make them public at the appropriate time, you will be safe. If I were you I would start looking for mining operations that are technically deserted but maintain traffic coming in and out. Then go for the mines where the minerals extracted don't match the type of equipment required, and so on. With the public eye interested in those operations the fronts will either fail, or they will implement drastic changes you will be able to study with your statistical analysis. A few of those mines are used as entrance points to tunnel systems where some of the creatures can interact with the planet's resources without drawing attention to themselves. Were they suddenly discovered, they could feel threatened enough to exterminate humans claiming their own safety was at risk. However, if the pressure over them is increased little by little, they will retreat more and more without a clear justification to attack humans in the eyes of the other alien races. Does this make sense to you? Step by step and without scaring them too much all of a sudden. Trust the albinos with white or blond hair, and be extremely careful with the small grey ones, but in any case no sudden moves that could alter the status quo too much.

I hope one day you can forgive me for all those countless times when your research was refused, pulled down from journals, or the online platforms you used for informal stuff hacked to keep your SEO results as low as possible.

In a way it is ironic that a man who dedicates his life to identifying patterns about everything, assumes that he himself is a victim of random events.

I know you will try to find me, and I don't blame you, but by the time this letter reaches you I will most likely have passed away. Please, don't judge me too harshly for thinking that secrets would protect society. I can see now that the right balance between unfiltered truth and total secrecy is the only way in which our planet can find the right path forward.

Kind regards from a friend who couldn't be.
A. K.

DIPLOMATIC MISSION

The middle-aged man finished dressing up in the strange clothes that had been selected for him a few days before, and collected the vase with the different insignias from all the nations that had agreed to be represented by him. Only six territories were absent in this mission: Tuvalu, Angola, North Korea, Kosovo, Switzerland, and the South Pole. One of the many surprises of the whole enterprise had been the fact that the North Pole had actually required representation. Many shocking things had happened in the weeks before the trip that was now about to take place. First on the list would probably have to be the fact that an intelligent life form had openly established contact with the different countries and autonomous territories that formed the political system of the planet. That fact alone should be surprising enough, but when the alien envoy informed everyone about his intentions of visiting the inhabitants of the North Pole, most nations thought it would be some mistake from an unaware foreign life form.

The shock came when over the space marked as North Pole, appeared a Nazi flag in blue and white. This mission had changed too many ideas about the reality of our planet. Aziz Jensen Rodríguez was the person chosen based on the criteria from the visitors. His parents coming from mixed families themselves had met at a cruise around the world, so it was as if from the start that kid had been overly well-positioned for the task at hand. Fascinated by diplomacy like his father, obsessed by history like his mother, and an overall nerd who was now being explained why on earth he was being forced to offer representation services to Nazis.

-Mr. Jensen... Let me assure you we are all as appalled as you are, but a refusal to include a territory that wishes to be represented could jeopardize this whole operation. You do realize this is a historical moment for all of us, for humanity, correct?
-I do, I really do... but how can I be expected to represent a culture that would have killed or imprisoned half of my family tree given the chance? Where did these North Pole Nazis come from?
-Well... This is classified information, as you can surely guess.
-I was under the impression that I had some clearance in order to avoid situations like these.
-Yes, you may very well have such clearance but...

-Oh! Let me guess. You have no idea yourself, right Senator?
-We have a few theories we are working on at the moment.
Nothing conclusive yet.
-So not only do I have to represent them in some other planet, I
am also supposed to solve mysteries now? Cool... Just cool.
-Mr. Jensen, I'm going to be frank with you. I have no idea why
these beings have selected precisely you, considering there are
plenty of diplomatic officials with more experience and better
qualifications. I expect you to remember that everyone is
replaceable if they fail.
-Replaceable? Maybe, but not by you. You are just another flag in
a huge... vase... Why a vase though? I wish someone could
explain me this kind of things. Anyway... don't fly too high
Icarus, or you will burn your wings. Threatening the person who
must represent your interests in front of those creatures is...
unwise.
-It is clear that you are way over your head with this
assignment.
-Hm... Who wouldn't be? I can open with something like: "Do you
know which nation was the first and only one to use nuclear
weapons against another nation?"
-I... Perhaps I... may have overstepped. We might have started
on the wrong foot here.
-Ah! On the other hand, World War II would have been a lot
longer and cost more lives without that display of military might
to end the conflict. Perhaps it's better to leave that part of
human history out for now.
-Yes... Thank you for your understanding.

Aziz kept walking towards another one of his meetings with the
different countries involved in the mission. The time allocated for
those meetings was agreed upon with the United Nations based
on a number of factors that boiled down to a combination of
population and engagement in the international political arena.

-Yes, yes... We understand but how are you going to explain
them the rich traditions and history of our land without any
materials? Sir, we have dozens of gods in the main religion of our

country- Explained the Indian representative.

-I know. I know that, but from what I have been told they have
been studying the history and cultures of this planet for some
time. Chances are they know more about your country than you,
Minister.

-Forgive me if I appear too bold and direct, but... What is the
point of sending a representative up there if they already know
everything about us?

-Certainly not going there to give history lessons. Is that what
your diplomats do when they visit a foreign country, Minister?

The silence filled the room for a bit. After a few more pointless
questions the time was finally over. The meetings with the
representatives of Turkey, Australia, and Vietnam went better
than expected. They didn't have any special requests but just a
general hope that these alien beings weren't violent or
destructive. They communicated their concerns in a brief manner
and wished Aziz good luck in his future endeavors.

Most of the representatives he met that week expressed a
common idea in one way or another: They would love to get a
closer look at the newcomers and their culture, but they didn't
envy the burden of carrying the diplomacy of more than 200
nations at the same time and in these circumstances. The
meeting room chosen for the "special cases" was a different one.
It reminded more of a conference hall for important signatures
than an office for conducting business. The representative from
the North Pole was already waiting. Aziz made a gesture for him
to be silent, placing his extended index finger in front of his lips
as he examined the room for spying devices and hidden bugs.
The blond long-haired man wearing a weird-looking loose shirt
didn't understand the gesture and started talking anyway.

-Hello. Am I speaking to the Ambassador Jensen?

-Yes... No, not an ambassador yet. Would you give me a moment
while I check something?

-Spies?

-Yeah, I guess in a way we could call them that.

-It's safe. We have checked.

-Ok then... So, whom do I have the pleasure of addressing?
-Counselor Francis Schmidt. It's a pleasure for me as well.

Despite their polite words, both men had a cold attitude towards each other. They would have preferred to be in any other place.

-To be honest, I always thought the North Pole was inhabited by penguins.
-And seals.
-Yeah... That too.
-And Saami, Inuit, Khanty, etc. As for us, I guess we could say we like to keep to ourselves.
-Indeed. Who are "us" exactly? Would this be a good time to explain me how did the Nazis conquer the North Pole without anyone knowing?
-But that's not accurate I am afraid. The Swabian Star has been visited by a few expeditions. Admiral Byrd did so in a few occasions. Do you know that name by chance?- The man took two glasses from his briefcase, and poured a blue liquid from an expertly crafted crystal bottle.
-Swabian Star? Is that the name of the nation you created up there? Correct me if I am wrong but Admiral Byrd talked mostly about the things he found at the South Pole.
-We know. We had access to his works just like you did.
-So... That would be a discrepancy, care to explain perhaps?

The condescending tone was accompanied by a hand gesture refusing the glass offered to him by counselor Schmidt.

-We had a very cordial relation with the admiral. He was kind enough to modify some details in his writings to avoid creating a difficult situation for us.
-Very kind of him indeed. So this cordial relation... Did it start before or after he was awarded dozens of medals for his service against the enemies of the free world?
-Would that be us? Is that the type of open-minded thinking you plan on bringing to this diplomatic mission?
-My great-grandmother died in the concentration camp of Treblinka.

-I am very sorry for your loss. Horrible things happen in a war.
My great-grandfather died in a gulag from the allies after years
of forced labor.
-The allies? The Soviets you mean. After you tried to invade their
country.
-I am sorry, perhaps I have been misinformed but wasn't the
Soviet Union part of the allies?
-I am almost certain my great-grandmother didn't try to invade
Russia in winter, or any other sovereign country for that matter.
-Tell me Mr. Jensen... Do you keep the same animosity towards
Italy? Japan? Current Germany? It's going to be hard to
represent all the countries you dislike.
-As far as I know they don't use the Nazi flag to represent their
nations.
-We changed the colors to represent our shift towards peaceful
times.
-And you kept the swastika to not lose contact with the murders
and the genocides, right? But hey... the colors are changed to
represent peace, so I guess the mixture is balanced after all.
-Why should we be forced to erase our history when you are
representing countries that use Communist flags to this day? Is
the life of their victims worth less to you?

For a second Aziz didn't have a clear comeback, but he hated the
idea of losing this discussion without at least trying his best.

-You see, counselor, when one loses a war and the world discover
the atrocities committed under that particular flag, created by
some particular man, it would be a good use of common sense to
change it completely. Even the Soviet Union changed its flag
when they separated to distance themselves from the mistakes of
that past.
-Ah. I was talking about China.

The tension in the room increased by moments, but Aziz knew
when he had ran out of options and decided to follow another
path that might prove more successful.

-Very well, counselor. You have the right to use any flag you desire if it is legal in your area of the world. Let's hope these aliens decide to organize the meeting there and not in Berlin or Jerusalem... otherwise you and I might be arrested and tried for wearing hate symbols.
-Perhaps we could cover the flag of my country with a Chinese one? I heard their concentration camps get a pass these days.
-Oh! Aren't you a sassy one, counselor? I don't think they are gassing children in China... like you used to do back in the day; remember? But ok. Moving on... How did you establish up there exactly?
-First of all I would appreciate it if you kept this conversation respectful. Secondly, I didn't use to do anything. I am more or less your age. Those things happened long before I was born, and it was one of the reasons why our people stopped contributing to the war effort.
-You say "our people"... I have a technical question. Am I representing Nazis? That would make "your people" and "the people who gassed children" the same people, wouldn't it?
-Would it also make current Japanese people the same people that tortured and experimented with prisoners of war? The things they did to those men were much more brutal than anything done anywhere else during that war. You seem to be ok representing them even though their flag has also changed very little. Double standards perhaps?
-That flag had centuries of history. It wasn't created by a genocidal maniac... But anyway, our time is limited and I doubt you want to spend it all talking about flags. How did you establish up there?

The man left the glass on the table and stared attentively at Aziz, trying to assess how much information he could share with the diplomat taking into account the blatant hostility he felt towards him and his country.

-The Swabian Star was the name of a group of military and scientific bases Germany established in the North Pole in order to grant a better control of Scandinavia. We operated in a semi-secret regime. Most powers assumed that if the Reich had such a strong interest in establishing bases in Antarctica, they most likely had already taken control of the Artic region... The North Pole.

-Yes, but how did that come to happen? And why has it been secret all this time?

-Secret for you Mr. Jensen. We haven't been a secret, but more of a discreet reality.

-Yeah, clear. Why though?

-Once the war was almost lost, many officers fled with their families up north. Argentina was too far away and too risky once Normandy proved to be a success for the Allies. The passage from Germany to Denmark, Norway, Finland, etc. was the alternative many chose. The protection of those German citizens became one of our main concerns. Some were in their early 20s and 30s when they relocated, so we thought it was prudent to wait until after the last inhabitant in danger had passed away before opening ourselves to public scrutiny. Decades after the war the Israeli intelligence service was still hunting down our fellow citizens.

-Hunting down as in "bringing them to justice for war crimes"?

-No Mr. Jensen. A big portion of those men weren't brought in front of any judge, but executed without giving them a chance to defend themselves. I am sure you feel no empathy for any of them. In your eyes they were all directing a crematory, but the reality is that many of them were just brainwashed kids that realized the horrors hidden within the Nazi regime even before the war finished. Operation Valkyrie, Rommel's assassination... The German people began to fight Hitler's rule as soon as they realized who he really was and what he had done.

-Aha, that... or basically they saw the war was lost and they wanted to surrender in better conditions as they admit in their interviews and books after the war. But if you prefer your sugarcoated version of the story, who am I to take that away from you? Could you finally tell me how you managed to keep that place a secret?

-It wasn't as hard as you might imagine. The bases were

designed as bunkers, raw materials were abundant throughout
the war, and some of the best German scientists were coming
and going all the time, until they finally established there. I am
not going to deny that lack of vitamin D is always a struggle, but
relatively similar to the situation in Svalbard, Northern Finland,
or Iceland.

Aziz examined the situation. Something didn't make much sense.
He couldn't still figure out what it was, but he felt he was being
played somehow.

-Do you still have relatives in Germany, counselor?
-Some cousins I would think. Why?
-It must be hard for everyone living in Swabian Star not to visit
their relatives.
-But they do. Fake passports aren't hard to come by these days.
-And what are those conversations like? They visit some uncle or
some cousin and what do they tell them? That they are living in
the North Pole helping Santa?
-Ahahahah! No, certainly not. We usually come up with stories
about having migrated to America, Canada, Norway, etc.
-Heh! Yeah, it must be hard to live in constant fear of one of
them getting drunk and spilling the beans about the secret,
right?
-Luckily it hasn't happened so far.-The counselor tried to keep a
jolly attitude but the questions were beginning to undermine the
narrative.
-May I see pictures of the place? I would like to see the people I
am representing. I hope that's ok.
-Certainly. I have some photos in my laptop. Most of them of our
typical celebrations, and some of my own family.

Aziz studied the images carefully. After a few of them a smile
appeared on his face.

-Interesting... Very interesting indeed.
-I am glad you find our celebrations interesting. I hope one day
you are able to visit them in person.
-Oh! I would hate to destroy the chromatic integrity of all these

pictures.

-What do you mean? I don't follow.

-Well, let me explain you then. Earlier in our conversation you mentioned how the Swabian Star got populated with "refugees" and scientists from all over Germany, are you following so far?

-Yes, what's your point exactly?

-Well, my point is that every single person in the pictures happens to have light hair... really light hair. Contrary to popular belief, only 46% of the German population has blond hair in the region where it is more common. In some regions the percentage goes down reaching less than 20% in Baden, Lusatia, or Bavaria...

The counselor began to look really nervous. He had prepared for most questions, but not for something like this. He could have gone for hours about submarine routes delivering scientific equipment and seeds to the colony. He could have described feasible ways in which a microclimate could have been achieved with the limited technology of the 1930s, but he had no explanation for the fact Aziz had noticed.

-Well... The fashion trends. You know. Everyone is dying their hair these days. Plus the lack of sun makes hair lighter, as you know.

-You sound much more convincing when you answer the questions you had prepared for our meeting. Improvising is not your thing, counselor. So your children also follow that fashion trend? And that trend started in the 1940s from what I can tell looking at the earlier pictures. Quite a persisting and unanimous fashion trend I must say.

-The... the thing is that...

-Oh! Yes? What thing? Tell me... And while you are at it, explain me this weird festival you have going on here. It certainly looks like a recreation of things one doesn't really understand. Look at the guy in this picture... What is he doing exactly? One chicken leg in his left hand, one cake in the other. That's not how we do things here on Earth. That other lady is...

A trembling counselor got up from his seat, ready to leave the room. Aziz held his shoulder and tried to push the situation further to his advantage.

-What's going on here? What are you trying to accomplish by pretending to be Nazis?
-I must go. Please, release me, or I will release myself.
-Oh! That would be perfect. Getting discovered and assaulting your representative! The perfect day for you counselor. Perhaps it would be wiser if you...

The man ignored the words and dashed for the door anyway, leaving some of his things behind. Aziz postponed the rest of the meetings until the next day, and prepared to analyze all the pictures and items the mysterious man had brought with himself.

-Well, well... Who are you Counselor Schmidt? What is going on? As if aliens visiting us wasn't weird enough we get fake Nazis in the North Pole.

The next day the meetings went as expected, but the proximity of the first encounter with the aliens made everyone nervous. Little by little everyone began to recognize how bad it looked when humans worldwide couldn't organize themselves with one voice to deal with other planets. It made us look divided and primitive in the eyes of civilizations that had no major difficulty agreeing on a common course of action that would benefit them all.

-Are you ready for this? If you have any problem up there, we will...
-You will what, director? It's not as if you can do much from here if they decide to take me on board, dissect me, or probe me from behind... One never knows.
-Hah! It's nice to see you keep your good mood intact. Let's all hope it doesn't come to that.
-Any last words of advice?
-Nope. None of what I learned in Madagascar or New Guinea could ever get close to what you are about to experience... Try not to offend them so they don't destroy the planet, ok?

-Will do. Thanks for everything, Jack. See you when I'm back... I hope.

The alien spaceship was nothing like Aziz had imagined. It had a circular shape made from a material whose texture seemed to change in a pattern of waves and light reflections. It would have been impossible to replicate that effect with our current technology. It was as if the surface of the ship interacted directly with the space around it instead of being affected by it. The object floated in front of him without any feasible way to access it, or a landing platform that allowed it to rest on the surface. It was levitating without producing any semblance of a sound, besides those of the wind currents being affected by its surface. Suddenly, one of the sensors in Aziz's suit began to beep.

-Control? It seems we have an alarm going off. What is this about? Do I approach the object?- The words were pronounced trying to hide the fear.
-Stop advancing Jensen. That's a radiation alarm. Whatever that thing is, it produces radioactivity of some kind. Approach the blue van behind you and suit up for an NBC scenario.
-Wait, a portal has opened in front of the ship. Some guy is coming out... He looks human. Do I proceed?
-Is the sensor still beeping?
-Not at this distance. The ship seems to be radioactive but the guy isn't.

As the figure approached Aziz realized it was a woman wearing clothes that were modern in style and seemed tailored.

-Ambassador Jensen. You may call me Eva. I will be the representative for the people that occupies two solar systems of what you named Canis Major. We don't use any name to refer to ourselves, but when we interact with other cultures we use terms adapted to their speech functions. Is the name Doosaree Kolonee comfortable for you? Doosarians?
-It's an honor to meet you Eva. Please call me Aziz. Yes, that term is easy for me to pronounce. Thank you for your kindness.- Aziz was measuring his every word in an effort to avoid making

any mistake.
-We have been studying your culture, but I apologize in advance
if I make any mistake.
-As do I. This is all new for me, and for the planet. The radio
devices are disconnected, soooo... this conversation will be
private.
-I thank you for your clarity, Aziz. This is not our first visit to the
planet as you know by now.
-With all due respect, what do you mean?
-Counselor Schmidt has already told me that you figured out our
small deception. I apologize in case our caution approaching the
colony of the Swabian Star could be interpreted as dishonest.
-But... why did you think it was necessary to lie about that
colony?
-We thought it would perhaps be more appropriate to present
Swabians as humans, instead of Doosarians. If this planet knew
there were aliens among them, they could consider them as
spies, or a threat, or something too worthy of attention. We
wanted to avoid droves of people being drawn to the Swabian
Star. I hope you can understand and forgive us.
-Yes of course. Don't mention it. I have a doubt though... Why did
you choose precisely me?
-We wanted a representative that had a mixed background of
cultures and experiences. That way we thought it would be
easier for different countries to feel identified in your
representation, rather than the representation of a person who
only "belongs" to one place.
-The fact that most of my ancestors are Jewish, didn't play a
part?

The Doosarian lady seemed to be taken aback for the first time
during the conversation. But she simply smiled briefly and
politely.

-Why have you come to Earth exactly?- Asked Aziz.
-A grave danger is about to befall this planet. We have been
guarding your steps for millennia and the time has come to play
a more active role in the management of planet Earth. We hope

our two cultures can benefit from an agreement in which we will do our best to guarantee the safety of your planet.
-I see. This danger you speak of... Could you be a bit more precise?
-An invasion of planet Earth by a hostile alien race. We need to be prepared before they strike. We need to work together and do our best to prevent a human extinction.
-Of course! Count on us! What would you need to achieve this goal?
-It will be a complex plan with many steps. The Juk'Yau aggressors are worried about the current nuclear capabilities of some nations. We need to decrease their justification for an attack. We will need to create a defense system that...
-That will be managed by you, right?
-Yes. Is that a problem?

Aziz went silent for a few seconds. Looked at his radioactivity sensor and to the woman in front of him. Then he started to see a clear picture of what was really going on.

-How did you do the portal thing though? That was impressive...
-You mean the technology?
-Yeah... the trick you used. That's what I mean. Excuse me, I'll be right back.- Aziz turned around and left the area, shocking the Doosarian lady in the process.

As he approached his director he made a hand gesture.

-Ah! So option B it is. You were right all along... I owe you a fancy meal I guess.
-Yep... Nuclear radiation in an advanced spaceship? I don't think so. Their plan is to make us believe there is an important threat only THEY can protect us against. Smoke and mirrors, director... Smoke and mirrors.
-This must be one of the weirdest episodes in human history... The Nazi colony from the North Pole that tried to rise to power pretending to be alien protectors. Crazy...
-Don't judge them too harshly. As surveillance technologies advance there are less and less places to hide. How long would it

be until they were found? They probably figured leaving in style was their best option.

-I wonder how they do their levitation and portal stunts. Those Nazi remnants have a few tricks up their sleeve apparently. A very bold move anyway.

The two men started walking away from the place as the local military arrested the woman and 12 other people in the surrounding area. The Swabian Star case would shake the international community for years to come.

THE END

18- 9- 3- 1- 18- 4- 15 // 18- 15- 17- 22- 5 // 13- 1- 21- 5- 15- 20